SAVING JESSIE'S GIRL

LAUREN BIEL

Library of Congress Cataloging-in-Publication Data

Saving Jessie's Girl/Lauren Biel 1st ed.

Cover Design: Laura Hidalgo of Spellbinding Design

Editing: Sugar Free Editing

Interior Design: Sugar Free Editing

For more information on this book and the author, visit: www.Lauren Biel.com

Please visit LaurenBiel.com for a full list of content warnings.

PLAYLIST

1. "Jessie's Girl" by Rick Springfield (on repeat)

This book is dedicated to the readers who found a reason to keep writing their stories

CHAPTER ONE

EMMY

Saturday nights are the worst. The bar puts on the game, and all the drunk patrons get a little too handsy for my liking. I don't mind if someone thinks whatever they want to think, but keep the comments and groping to yourself, you know? As a server, I'm expected to smile and pretend I'm okay with constant sexual harassment. HR who? Never met her.

My coworker bustles over and shoves a tray of food into my hand. "Run this to table two, and watch out. The dad is a douchebag."

She dashes off without so much as thanking me, but that's okay. I'm the new girl here, having only been here a few weeks, so I guess this is some form of hazing. They keep pawning the worst of the worst onto me.

As I approach table two, the man in question rolls his eyes before I've even set down the first plate of food. He studies each meal as it's placed down, searching with scrutinizing eyes for something, anything that may be incorrect. And he finds it.

"I told that girl I wanted yellow mustard!" He plucks the ramekin of honey mustard from his plate and chucks it at the floor. The sauce cup topples over my shoes, probably staining the laces. Just my fucking luck. "I've been waiting for over an hour already!"

I check the ticket. It's been just over twenty minutes, but okay.

"So sorry about that," I say with a smile as I bend to retrieve yellow mustard's inferior cousin from the floor. "I'll be right out with the correct sauce."

I offer smiles to his wife and bratty child, expecting a little sympathy from them, but they just scowl at me.

Honestly, fuck him and his honey mustard. I'm more concerned about what the yellow sauce will do to my white sneakers, so I hurry to the bar. The last thing I need is to be sent home because I'm not up to snuff, and Dale, our boss, cares about what his girls look like on the floor. Besides, I won't get the tip from that table anyway.

Behind the bar, I fill a cup with soda water and grab a rag from the bin. Then I hurry to the dark corner where we usually prep silverware for the next day's service. I pull off my shoe and set to work, scrubbing and hoping no one sees this health-code violation. My eyes dart around, making sure none of the other staff have noticed me, and that's when my gaze lands on table five.

Rule number one in waitressing: don't make eye contact with other tables. If you do, someone will inevitably want something from you, and as fate would have it, that's exactly what happens.

A hand rises in my direction, and I try to ignore it. Can't those men see that I'm currently down a shoe and scrubbing like my life depends on it? I look down at the stains, which are little more than ghosts of themselves now. In this low lighting, surely no one will notice. I shove the shoe over my foot and hurry to their table.

"How can I help?" I ask the two men.

They look similar. Both have dark hair and piercing blue eyes, so I can only assume they're related. The one in the polo looks like he breaks hearts for a living, and the other one looks like he breaks faces. They're both good-looking men—*very* good-looking, just in different ways. One dresses in a polo and khakis, the other in jeans and a band t-shirt. One rocks a hairstyle just messy enough to know it took at least fifteen minutes to perfect. The other's hair hangs over his right eye, with an edgy undercut to really sell the bad-boy vibe.

The one in the band t-shirt opens his mouth, but nothing comes out. Still, I get a glimpse of a tongue piercing. Coupled with the black septum piercing and those black spider bites, I can only imagine what it would be like to—

Oh, jeez, stop it, Emmy!

The pierced man begins signing to his brother. He tells him to ask for another water.

"One water, coming up," I say, and both men turn toward me, shocked. "My brother is deaf, so I learned ASL," I sign.

"He's not deaf," the man in the polo says. "He can't talk."

"No worries there," I say. "I talk enough for everyone."

I scurry off to prepare a water, and as I approach the table, I study the men again. Yes, definitely brothers. The face shape is too similar to be anything else. Possibly twins?

"Here's your water," I say as I slide the glass toward the pierced guy, and he nods.

"I'm Jessie, and that's Benji," the polo shirt—Jessie—says. "What's a pretty girl like you doing in a place like this?"

"This is my second job, actually. I'm also a stripper."

Benji chokes on the water, spewing it across the table.

"I'm kidding," I say, much to Jessie's dismay. His smile falters. "I'm a failed real estate agent by day, bar whore by night."

"The market is ice-cold right now, but it always warms back up," Jessie says. "Don't worry, it will get better."

His words comfort me. Or maybe it's just that he's so damn attractive. Either way, I feel a little better.

"Thanks," I say. "Do you guys need anything else?"

Before they can respond, one of my coworkers sidles up to me and pulls her order pad from her apron. "Sorry about that, boys. Are you ready to order?" She glances at me, clearly giving me the brushoff, and I don't blame her. I'd want this table all to myself too.

I turn to leave, but Jessie's hand whips out and wraps around my arm.

"Wait, you didn't get my number yet," he says with a sly smile. He motions for my coworker to give him a slip of paper from her notepad, and she does. With another scowl at me. He jots something down, then slides it into my hand. "Call me."

I usually wouldn't accept a number from a stranger, but maybe the real estate market isn't the only thing in need of warming up right now. I stuff the paper into my apron and hurry off. Maybe I won't call him.

But maybe I will.

CHAPTER TWO

BENJI

The drive back to the apartment is quiet for once. You'd think that with my inability to speak aloud, it would always be quiet, but no. Jessie usually fills the silence with his incessant talking or loud music. It's nice to have a moment to think.

I love my twin brother, don't get me wrong, but he's a lot. I love him, but I can't say that I like him very much.

And one of the reasons why appears on our right.

"Oh shit, is that Harvey?" Jessie says as he sits a little straighter in the driver's seat. "If it is, we gotta flag him down."

Harvey is Jessie's favorite coke dealer, and coke is Jessie's favorite drug. He's what you call a coke snob, thumbing his powdered nose at the other addicts as if he isn't one of them. Coke is the drug of the wealthy and powerful, he says. I guess that's why I never got into it. He's both of those things, and I'm neither.

Jessie takes care of both of us since it's hard for me to

find work with my inability to speak in a way that the majority of the population understands. On the surface, he looks like the perfect brother. If it weren't for the hate in his heart, he might have been just that.

He pulls the black truck to the side of the road and shouts for Harvey. The man ventures closer and pulls a baggie from his pocket, already knowing what Jessie needs. As they're completing the transaction, another of Harvey's regulars shows up. We've seen her a few times before, but I've never gotten her name.

"You buying for everyone tonight?" she says with a flirty smile toward Jessie. The flirty smiles aren't always directed at him, but once the women realize I'm different, they lose interest and go for the verbal brother.

Jessie smiles back and gives her a wink. "Maybe. You free tonight? We have room in the cab if you want to take a ride."

My hackles rise. Jessie and coke are a bad enough combination, but when you toss a woman into the mix, it's bound to get downright volatile.

I tug Jessie's arm and start signing, but he doesn't spare me a glance. That's something the speaking don't have to worry about. If someone doesn't want to listen, they don't often have a choice, but avoiding sign language is as simple as closing your fucking eyes.

The girl spares me a nervous glance. "What's his problem?"

"He's just jealous that I get all the pretty girls. Hop in." Jessie pats the middle seat between us, and I roll my eyes.

He gets all the pretty girls because I haven't really tried to take one for myself. If I found a woman worth having, I might find the fucks to give, but so far, no one has turned my head enough. Getting my dick wet has never been an issue. Finding the will to care about another human, though? I don't have it in me. Or rather, I don't have it in me *anymore*. My voice wasn't the only thing I lost as a child.

With the deal done, the girl climbs into the cab, and I fight for my next breath. She smells like she bathed in a tub filled with perfume from CVS. All of them. I can't even pick a scent from the amalgamation of flowers currently assaulting my sinuses.

I roll the window down and suck in fresh air as we cruise down the street. At least the cute girl from the bar hasn't called my brother. Maybe if I sneak down there without him one evening, I can have a conversation with her. Maybe that will to give a fuck isn't completely squashed after all.

Minutes later, we pull into the parking lot at my apartment. Jessie doesn't even bother getting out of the truck before he encourages her to pull out her baggie so they can do a quick bump before heading in. Typical Jessie. He makes sure to fuck every woman at least twice—once in the bedroom, and again where her drugs are concerned.

I get out of the truck before he can beg me to join them. Despite the way I look, all rough around the edges, I'm a pretty straight-laced guy. I don't enjoy the way drugs make me feel, and I definitely don't enjoy treating women like trash. Those are two of Jessie's favorite pastimes.

Just as I flop onto the couch, they stumble in through the door. They're all smiles right now. I wonder how long this will last.

"Do a line with us," he says, and he's already pulling his baggie from his pocket.

It's not surprising that I know him so well. He's my twin brother, after all.

He wiggles the tiny bag in front of my face and raises his eyebrows. "Eh? You know you want to have a little fun."

His idea of fun is getting high enough to excuse whatever pain he plans to inflict. I can handle it, but I'm not so sure about the girl. She looks like she's been roughed up enough for one lifetime.

She hasn't been around long enough to put two and two together, though. As Jessie spreads some powder on the table and breaks it into four lines, she doesn't seem to understand that combining Jessie and coke is like holding a match to a powder keg. Someone is bound to get hurt in the coming explosion.

But I say nothing as they lean over the table and inhale that white dust into their noses. Not that I could say anything if I wanted to.

I hear everything just fine. My brain processes sound, and I can formulate a response. But when the response reaches my vocal cords, it goes no further. Like a bull calf caught in a squeeze pen, my throat closes up and chops off my voice, rendering me sterile. That's how it feels to me, anyway.

The girl bends at the waist to suck up another line. It's been just long enough for the first bump to reach Jessie's brain and start tickling that spot that gets him riled up. I see it in his eyes, in the way they widen and lock-in on the girl. His hand shoots forward and wraps around her upper arm, snatching her backward. She winces as his fingers dig into her in a way they shouldn't.

"Quit being a greedy little bitch," he snarls. "That's for my brother, and the last line is for me."

I roll my eyes. "I don't want any. Let her have it."

"What's he saying with his hands?" she asks. She makes a bunch of nonsense motions with her fingers.

"He's mute. He's saying that he wants you to take off your fucking clothes and give him a lap dance." Jessie smirks, then flashes that million-dollar smile that gets him all the girls. He has a nasty habit of saying I said things I didn't say. "Isn't that right, Benji?"

The girl looks between us, and her confidence has taken a hit. Oh, *now* she's scared. It's too bad those warning bells weren't ringing before she climbed inside his truck.

I sit back with a sigh as he leans forward and takes both lines from the table. When he's done, he leans back and wipes his nose, sniffing a few times to really get that shit into his brain.

My eyes drift to the girl. Jessie is busy analyzing something on his phone—probably porn—so I do my best to tell her just how unsafe she is. I look from her to the door, but she's too high or too stupid to get the hint.

Finally, Jessie lowers the phone and looks the girl dead in the face. "You can get out now."

"What?" She leans back a little.

I roll my eyes.

"Get the fuck out," he says, but this time, he grabs her arm again. "You tried to steal a line, and I don't like greedy bitches."

"That was like, fifteen minutes ago!" she screeches.

Oh boy. This isn't going to be pretty. He really doesn't like it when women respond. I call it conversation. He calls it disrespect.

He raises his arm and backhands the girl so hard that she crumples to the floor. I have to do something. If I don't stop him, he'll put her in the hospital . . . the part of the hospital where they shove you into a drawer and call your next of kin to identify you.

I jump to my feet and get between them. Jessie is

already standing over her as she cowers on the floor and looks up at him like she can't believe he's done this.

"Let her go," I sign.

Jessie shakes his head and scoffs. "Hell no. Someone's getting their ass beat tonight. It's either her or you."

God, I hate that we share the same DNA.

"Tell her to leave, and we'll fight it out," I sign.

Jessie's eyes burn a hole in my face. "Get out," he says to her without his piercing blue eyes leaving me. "I'll call you tomorrow."

The girl scrambles to her feet and hurries out of the apartment without so much as a backward glance. The worst part? He will absolutely call her tomorrow, and she'll answer.

As soon as the door clicks shut, Jessie is on me. This is all he wanted. A fight. Some simple, animalistic way to vent his frustrations. This is how it usually goes when he tosses coke into the mix. Not that he needs a reason.

I throw a few swings, but there's no heat behind them. The part of the punching bag is mine to play and has been for as long as I can remember. Each time we fight, I hold back. I'm not afraid of Jessie, and if I really wanted to, I could fuck him up far worse than what he does to me. But the goodness and loyalty that Jessie lacks had to go somewhere, and I ended up with all of it. Whenever possible, I step in and take the beating. Better me than the girls.

I keep my head tucked low as he wails on me. My face is one of the few things I have going for me, and I don't want to fuck it up. My brother and I look a lot alike—dark hair, blue eyes, a jawline that drops panties. That's where the similarities stop. He is a grade-A asshole, and I'm . . . not.

To look at us, though, you'd think the bad attitude would have come to me. I'm the one with the multitude of piercings, both facial and otherwise. He's the clean-cut type. That's the trouble with judging a book by its cover. Sometimes you miss the good stories and end up with the shitty ones.

Jessie's fist drives into my ribs a final time before he lets up and steps back. His chest heaves with his efforts, and the fire in his eyes challenges me to move. I don't. Not even to ask if he's finished.

"Don't you ever try to stop me from training a bitch again, do you hear me?"

"They aren't animals. They're people." I drop my hands and wait for the blow, but it doesn't come.

Jessie sighs and flops down on the couch, his rage spent for the moment. "Come on. Let's watch the fight. I hear it's gonna be a good one tonight."

He grabs the remote from the coffee table and props his feet in its place like he wasn't just beating me senseless. I'm not really in the mood to be around him right now, but if I don't occupy him, he might go in search of someone who will. At least until he comes down and crashes, I'll keep an eye on him.

This is how it's always been, even before the coke addiction. Jessic doesn't need the drugs to be mean. He just is. It's written in his DNA, and I'm grateful the pen wasn't lowered to my genetic parchment. I have no desire to hurt people. Including him.

So, I do what I've always done. I silently sit and wait for something to change. Because even though I love my brother, I hate who he is.

CHAPTER THREE

I'm a bundle of nerves as I wait outside the restaurant. Cars occasionally drift past, and a few people shuffle by on the sidewalk. I glance at each face, searching for my date, but I don't see him yet. *Maybe I'm just a little early*, I think, but when I look at my watch, it's twenty past when we were supposed to meet. I've been here for thirty minutes already.

This was a terrible idea. I never should have reached out to that guy from the other night. Jessie Rinehart. We made plans yesterday afternoon to meet tonight, but I guess I should have double-checked to make sure our plans still stood. I just didn't want to seem overeager. I mean, the guy is fucking hot.

A red sports car pulls up and straddles the handicap parking spot directly in front of me. I expect the driver to back up and straighten out, but they don't. The engine cuts off, and the door swings open. I almost say something as a man glides out of the car and brushes back his dark hair, but I swallow my tongue.

It's Jessie.

He looks good in a navy button-down and slacks. Maybe he didn't realize that was a handicap spot. I let it go for now, not wanting to ruffle feathers.

"Hey, beautiful," he says as he pulls a rose from behind his back. I'm more of a carnation girl, but this is okay too. He kisses my hand and firmly wraps his arm around my waist. "Hope I didn't keep you waiting too long."

"Just half an hour, no biggie," I say with a nervous laugh.

He brushes past this and guides me into the restaurant. A hostess seats us at a table by the window, and I feel so out of place among the suits and designer handbags. I'm more of a Longhorn girl for the first date, but Jessie chose this place.

The hostess tells us our server will be right with us, and I peruse the menu as we wait. It's like reading a foreign language because it *is* a foreign language. I don't understand a single thing, but I can't tell him that. I already feel uncouth. I do recognize the words ravioli and alfredo, so those seem like safe bets.

The server comes by and offers us a bottle of wine. I decline, but Jessie requests a glass for each of us. The red liquid burbles into the glass as the server smiles and asks if we've decided or if we need help.

"Anything the lady wants," Jessie says with a beaming smile.

Anything? Well, I'm not used to that. I've never had the money for a lot, let alone "anything."

"I'll have the ravioli alfredo," I say.

Jessie orders something I can't pronounce, and she nods and files it away in her mind before scurrying to the kitchen.

Now that the menus have been removed, I find I have nowhere to look but at my date. It's not a bad view. He seems to enjoy what he sees as well. He raises his wine to his lips, hardly able to contain his smile as he sips.

"You look stunning tonight," he says, lowering his glass.

My cheeks flush, and I swat away the compliment. "Compared to what I looked like at work the other night, I can see how you'd consider this an improvement. But you don't look too shabby yourself."

He preens under the praise, licking his perfectly shaped lips and leaning forward. "I can't wait to finish this meal so I can take you back to my place."

I give him a smirk. I'm not the type of girl you can take home on the first date, but I'm not against letting him try. "A bit presumptuous, aren't we?"

He smiles. "I wouldn't call it presumptuous. Just . . . confident."

Confidence is never a bad thing, but there's no way he's getting in my pants tonight. Now, the second date might be a different story . . .

As we wait for our meals to arrive, we chat about work. I learn that he's a higher-up in some tech firm, and he already knows what I do, so my side of the conversation doesn't last very long. Which is fine. I'm not too keen to talk about wait-ressing. Or my past.

By the time our food arrives, my stomach is growling. I haven't eaten a thing since lunch. I pluck up my fork, but Jessie's hand lands over mine.

"Manners, Emmy," he says with a flirty smile. "Your napkin goes in your lap. Then you wait for me to begin before you pick up your fork."

With a giggle, I play along. He has to be joking. No one takes etiquette that seriously anymore. I lower my fork, drape the napkin over my lap, and nibble my lip as I wait for him to proceed. Maybe this is some kinky form of dominance foreplay.

"Sorry, I'm just *so* hungry," I say.

"You're hungry, huh?" he says with a sinful smirk. He takes a bite and motions for me to begin eating.

I've never tasted food like this. The pasta has just the right texture, and the sauce tastes of fresh cream and heaven. While I can't be sure what meat is inside each bite of ravioli, I *can* say that it's cheesy and delicious. The conversation blossoms between bites of pasta and sips of wine. We talk about what we like to do in our spare time—I like to binge reality TV; he likes to wakeboard on the lake, golf with friends, and watch UFC. We don't exactly have a lot in common on the surface, but opposites attract, right?

Eventually, the conversation moves to family. I learn that my assumption was correct, and that the man from the other night is, in fact, his twin brother. Before I can tell him about my brother and two sisters, he pushes on about how hard it's been to care for his mute sibling. My brother is deaf, and while we've never had to care for him—he's completely self-sufficient and does life better than I do—being differently abled comes with challenges. I'm so impressed with how he helps his brother.

"Why doesn't your brother speak?" I ask after a sip of wine. I should slow down, though. Despite the ravioli being delicious, there wasn't very much of it. All this wine on a nearly empty stomach is a recipe for danger.

Jessie shrugs. "Some kind of trauma. One day when we were kids, he just stopped talking and never spoke another word." He waves it off, ever the strong one. "He didn't say, so I didn't ask."

My heart sinks. That's so sad.

"Are you ready for the check?" the waitress asks, sneaking up on us and making me jump.

Jessie nods and takes the check before I can reach for it. Then he pulls out a black AmEx and shoves it inside the tidy leather book. I've never been on a date where I didn't pay my share. It feels . . . weird. I start fumbling through my clutch to give him cash, but he puts his warm hand over mine to stop me.

"Hey, I've got it." He offers another sly smile that makes my toes curl. "You just sit there, drink your wine, and look pretty. And if you won't let me take you back to my place, at least let me drive you home."

The wine must have gotten to me, because I agree. It's probably best I don't climb onto a bus in this state.

I follow him to his red sports car and climb inside. The butter-smooth leather melds with my ass the moment I sit down. I run my hand over the dash, enjoying the luxury. Who knew there was this much money in tech?

I give him my address. My head begins to swim as we take familiar turns. What was in that wine? Fucking Valium? I feel so tired.

After a few more traffic lights, we reach my place. Jessie helps me to the door. He pretty much has to with the way I'm stumbling around.

"You didn't warn me you were a lightweight," he says with a smirk as he supports my arm. "I hope you don't think I was trying to get you drunk."

I wave him off and try to find the key to my apartment, but they're all so blurry. "It doesn't usually hit me this hard."

The key finally slides into the lock, and I nearly fall inside the entryway. Jessie steps forward to steady me yet again. When he asks if I need help getting into bed, I start to say no, but who am I kidding? I can hardly walk. Besides, if he were going to try anything sideways, he wouldn't have asked.

We head toward my bedroom. He helps me undress, and he's a complete gentleman, so I do something I usually don't. I ask him to stay the night.

He says yes, and that's the last thing I remember.

CHAPTER FOUR

BENJI

Someone has been keeping my brother very occupied for the last few weeks. He's abandoned me near entirely, which means it's more than just one of his flings. I've hardly seen him at all. I wondered if it was that dark-haired chick from the other night, but something tells me it's someone a little more "high class."

Jessie doesn't mind bringing the coke angels to my apartment on the wrong side of town. It doesn't embarrass him. But when the girl is a little harder to convince, he puts on a show for as long as possible. Just until the hook is set and it's a little harder to get away. He's got it down to a science, and it's one subject I have no interest in.

Tonight he's decided to introduce me to her. He figured a bar off Main Street would be a good place, so we've secured a pool table in the back. He grabs a stick off the wall and checks to be sure it's level.

"Where's your date?" I sign.

"Running late," Jessie says with a shrug. "We can get started without her."

Always the gentleman. Sigh. Whoever she is, she's *so* lucky she picked Jessie. Cue the fucking eye roll.

He racks the balls and tosses a pool stick to me. "That girl . . . she's so good in bed, Benji. I might have to keep this one around a little longer than usual."

I set the stick by the table before signing, "I don't want to know about your sex life." I hope my fingers do what my voice can't, which is relay how uncomfortable he makes me when he talks about what was probably a private moment for the woman involved.

"Dude, what's the point of having a brother if I can't share the fun things with you?" He breaks, then lines up a shot and sinks two solids.

"You can share things with me. Just not those things." I watch him flub the next shot. "Whoever the girl is, she probably wouldn't like it very much."

"Oh, fuck you, Benji. You act like I don't know how to treat a woman right. And besides, would she keep coming back for more if I was a shitbag?"

I nod, but he doesn't see it. Something about him keeps women coming back. Is it the abuse? Maybe the misery? But he doesn't care, so I drop it. Whoever she is, it's not my business.

The door swishes behind me, and Jessie perks up as someone enters the pool hall. As he skirts around me to greet them, I spin and see Emmy, that pretty waitress from the bar. My brain doesn't put two and two together until he embraces her and leans down for a kiss.

My stomach shrivels in my gut, and my heart ceases to beat. *Not Emmy. Anyone but Emmy.*

As they part, she breezes closer, and it's like that

moment of sun between storm clouds. Her body is a dream in snug jeans and a black t-shirt that falls off her shoulder, but I'm solidly locked in on her beaming smile. And her eyes? God, they're like jewels the way they shimmer.

"Hey, Benji! Nice to see you again," she says.

"Good seeing you too. How've you been?" I sign.

She shrugs and looks up at Jessie as he winds his snake-like arm around her waist. "Can't complain. How about you?"

"I'm good."

I am not good. I am the exact opposite of good now that I know she's his current fixation.

I have *never* wanted one of his conquests. I've always cared about what happened to them, sure, but I've never desired to touch who he's touched. But even if she's been tainted by him, I've never wanted anyone more.

The worst part? I have no clue why.

She's beautiful, but her appearance isn't what has me in a chokehold. It can't be her personality. Hell, I've only been around her for ten minutes if you include what little time we saw her at the bar. No, there's something there. Some pull I can't deny.

But I'll have to deny it.

Jessie says something to her, but I can't hear him over the loud music and the clack of balls on the table next to us. Emmy shakes her head in response to whatever he says. She hasn't learned the rules yet, I see. You never tell Jessie no.

I take a drink of my beer as he grips her arm a little tighter, his words a little more insistent this time. My heart shatters the moment she turns around, engrossed in some kind of insta-argument with my brother. His face turns that pink hue that tells me he's getting annoyed. Time to play referee.

I stand and slide between them, shoving my pool stick into Emmy's hand. "You can take my turn."

Jessie rolls his eyes, knowing I'm ruining his plot to domineer this woman completely. "I gotta piss," he says before shoving his stick into my hand. "You can play while I'm gone."

Emmy turns away from me and swipes her eyes. The moment of sunshine has been traded for a dark, stormy cloud moving in to smother it. Her entire demeanor has flipped. She sits on a barstool and leans the stick against the wall.

I step closer to Emmy. "He's a dick sometimes. Don't let it ruin your fun."

"Kind of hard not to." She fiddles with a napkin on the table, then looks at me. "Is it me? Is something wrong with me?"

I shake my head and sit across from her. "No," I sign. "Nothing wrong with you. He's just . . ." My hands hesitate, unsure of what I want to say. "He's difficult."

Her face falls. "I was kind of hoping it was something I could fix about myself. That would be easier than hearing he's just this way."

This isn't helping, so I change the subject. "How'd you get that scratch on your arm?" I regret the question the moment it leaves my mouth, as that scratch might have come from some other miserable memory, but I'm grateful when a smile brightens her eyes.

"My kitten did that. Her name is Lily. She's actually over at your brother's house right now. I've been spending a lot of time there."

"The little gray kitten?" I sign. "I met her! I didn't know she was yours. I thought my brother finally found a soft spot for something other than himself."

I'm being an asshole, but it's true.

"Yeah, she's mine," she says. "She's driving Jessie nuts."

"Good," I sign, and we both laugh. I push the pool stick into her hand again. "Why don't you play my side? Get your mind off things. I'm stripes."

"I don't think Jessie wants me to play."

"I don't think it really matters what he wants." I shrug and motion for her to go for it.

She takes the pool stick and stands beside the table. I take her seat and watch as she lines up a shot, but she doesn't have a chance to take it before my brother appears again. When he sees the change of players, his lips turn down in a frown.

"Hand it back," he says to her. "I was trying to play a game with my brother."

"I'll take the winner," I sign. "Let her play."

Jessie tips his head back with an exaggerated groan. "Fine, but we have to start over."

He racks the balls again, and Emmy offers to break. Jessie waves her off and refuses to let her try. What do women see in him? I would have taken a step back and let her give it a go, but he just brushes her aside and sends the white ball into an explosion of color and sound. It doesn't stop there, though. Since he sank two balls, it's still his turn. He walks around the table, explaining every possible shot. I have to cover my mouth to hide a smirk when he misses entirely once he finally takes one.

"My turn?" Emmy asks.

Jessie nods and steps back, and she approaches the table. With an adorable wiggle of her hips, she sends the cue ball down the rails and sinks two stripes. I lean back and clap for her as Jessie pins me with a glare.

"Beginner's luck," he says. "Maybe we should get a lottery ticket after this."

"Maybe," Emmy says, and I don't miss the way Jessie bristles. She'll pay for that later. Jessie expects enthusiasm from his woman, no matter what he suggests.

She doesn't have a good shot, so she knocks the ball to an even worse spot for Jessie. He starts circling the table as Emmy wanders over to me. Her gaze lands on me for a moment, and I lift my hands to sign before she can look away.

"Who taught you how to play?"

Instead of speaking, she signs back. "My father was a professional pool player. He taught me a thing or two before he ran off."

My eyebrows rise as we share a moment. Or maybe it isn't shared so much as experienced by me. I'm not used to someone speaking my language. Even people close to me use their voice instead of ASL, so it's nice to have a conversation that feels like we're on equal footing. But this moment also renders me speechless. How terrible to finally have someone to talk to when I can't think of a fucking thing to say.

My cheeks flush, and I decide now is the perfect time for a quick smoke escape. It's Emmy's turn again, so I slip outside and light up. Silvery smoke rises from the end, keeping me distracted. When I finish, I light up another.

I'm avoiding going back inside. It's clear that I have a thing for my brother's girlfriend, and that can't happen. This need to protect her from him will be harder to squash than my feelings, though. I just don't know how I can warn her off. Ideally before he puts a mark on her.

I brush a hand through my dark hair and take a final

drag before squelching the second cigarette beneath my black combat boots. They feel like lead weights on my feet as I head back inside the bar. Emmy and Jessie no longer stand by the tables. I spot the top of my brother's head near the bathrooms, so I step closer. That's when I finally see Emmy's face.

I can't hear what he's saying, but based on the tears in her eyes, it's not very nice. She waves her hands, chin up as she defends herself. My eyes lock on Jessie's rising hand, and I rush around the corner. I know that gesture all too well. I curse myself immediately. Maybe this is what she needs to see to get her away from him, but I can't let him hurt her.

"What's going on?" I sign.

Jessie grunts. "Emmy's ready to go back to my place, and I'm not."

"I can drive her home," I sign.

"No, it's okay." Emmy grips her purse strap and looks toward the door. "I can just take the bus. Again."

"What's that supposed to mean?" Jessie bellows.

My hands move in a flurry. "Your place is on my way home. Just let me take her."

Jessie glances around, his eyes landing on a pretty blonde at the bar. He clears his throat. "You'll go straight home? No detours?"

She looks at the floor. "No detours."

Jessie pulls her against his broad chest. "Sorry I gave you shit. Send me the link to that dress you were looking at earlier. I'll have it delivered to my house, okay?" He lifts her chin. "I love you, Emmy Lewis. More than anything. You know that, right?"

She nods. They always nod.

As we head toward the exit, I'm annoyed that she doesn't seem upset by what happened tonight. What I stopped from happening. That's my brother, though. Full of faux apologies, love-bombs, and meaningless gifts.

We step into the night air and head for my car. It's a piece of shit compared to Jessie's sports car and luxury truck, but it's mine. I worked at a meat-packing plant for an entire summer to save up for it. Jessie didn't mind helping me cover an apartment, but a car? That was a bridge too far for him. I later realized that was because the apartment keeps me out of his hair, but a car for Benji benefits him not at all.

Before I turn the car on, I tap her arm and draw her eyes to me again. It's not easy to drive and sign, so I want to ask her this question before we get going.

"What were you two fighting about?"

Emmy shakes her head, sighs, and drops her head back against the seat. "Your brother thinks Dale is some other guy. I mean, he is a guy, but he's just my boss. I hate him, actually."

I nod and start the car. I can't really say much as I drive in the dark, but she seems like she just needs to talk anyway, so I'm happy to listen.

"I mean, he texted me tonight, but it was just about my shift tomorrow. Jessie saw it, and it set him off. He thinks Dale is being flirty and that he shouldn't text me at all. I think the beer is just getting to Jessie a bit."

A bit? A lot. The smallest amount of alcohol seems to set off sparks of anger inside that man. I can only assume he hasn't shown her evidence of his other little habit yet.

"I don't think he means to yell . . ." she continues.

I'm screaming inside, even if I can't on the outside. I want my voice to work so I can tell her that he absolutely means it, and he will only get worse. It's maddening. I will the muscles in my throat to work, but everything clamps down like it always does. My desperation is just not desperate enough, I guess. Or maybe I'm just as broken as our father said.

I pull up outside Jessie's house after winding through neighborhood streets. He lives in the nicer part of town, where sirens and gunshots are unheard of. Meanwhile, they're my lullaby every night.

Emmy searches through her purse, but her shoulders drop after a few seconds. "Fuck, I think I forgot the key he gave me. Do you have a spare?"

I shake my head. My brother doesn't want me dropping by unexpectedly, so he's never given me a key. He's always said if he wants to be around me, he'll find me.

I tap her shoulder, then sign, "I could take you to your place. I don't mind."

She nibbles her lip and closes her eyes. "This *is* my place. Your brother convinced me to move in with him a few days ago. He said it's better this way because I can save my money, and he can cover the bills."

I wince internally. He's moving fast with her. Too fast. It's better this way for Jessie, as it forces the woman to depend so fully on him for everything. It makes it harder for her to leave.

"I can't tell him I forgot my key. He'll be so pissed." She drops her head against the seat and blinks up at the roof of the car. "What the fuck am I supposed to do?"

"Come back to my place?" I sign. "I'll talk to him for you."

What I mean is, I'll take the beating for you, but I don't say that.

Emmy nibbles her lip and thinks. "Okay," she signs.

I put the car in reverse and head toward my apartment. I'll probably regret this, but I can't think about that right now.

CHAPTER FIVE

EMMY

Benji pulls into a dark parking lot in a very bad part of town. I only know it's a bad part of town because I lived over this way a few days ago. How odd that Jessie said it wasn't fit for a girl like me, but he's fine with his brother staying here.

Then again, I doubt anyone would fuck with Benji, regardless of his lack of voice. The piercings alone are unnerving. With the two black spider bites gleaming beneath the right side of his lower lip and that black septum ring, he looks like everything I was told to avoid all my life.

He steps out of the car and lights a cigarette. Holding it in his lips, he signs, "I don't like smoking in the car. Makes everything stink."

"Ever thought of quitting?"

He takes a drag and looks up at the moon, thinking. "Just thought about it, and it doesn't sound like much fun."

This pulls a laugh out of me, in spite of my sour mood.

Benji squelches what remains of the cigarette and motions for me to follow him inside.

"How long have you lived here?" I ask as I look around the space.

"Three years," he signs.

It sure doesn't look like it. Bare white walls glare at me from all sides. A decent-sized flatscreen stands on what must have been an old kitchen table with the leaves knocked off. Aside from that, a small couch, and a battered coffee table, the place is empty. It looks more like he's squatting than living here.

He must see the way I'm staring, because he signs, "My brother cares about appearances. Me? Not so much." He shakes his head, exaggerating the final words. Then he holds up his finger and smiles as he hurries to another room. He returns with a small picture frame, which he places on the coffee table. "There. A little homier now?"

"Oh, yes. That's just the touch it needed," I say, and we both laugh. His is nearly silent, but I get the sentiment.

I sit on the couch and pull the picture a little closer. They're much younger, and Benji hasn't gotten his piercings yet, but I can still tell the two of them apart.

"Where was this taken?" I ask. "The background looks familiar."

Benji's eyes light up. "The pier on the far side of town. The one by the lake where kids jump off the rocks."

"Hey, I've been there," I say as I slide the picture back to the center of the table. "I used to go and just sit on the pier and watch the boats slide by."

"Me too," he signs. "That was the last time Jessie took me. I don't really do much on my own. Too much trouble."

"Well, we'll just have to change your mindset and get you out more."

Benji smirks, and it does something to my insides that it absolutely shouldn't. "I'd like that."

The conversation stalls, so he tosses the TV remote into my lap and signs for me to put something on while he fetches some pillows and a blanket. I've decided on a comedy special by the time he returns.

"You can take my bed if you'd prefer," he signs.

I pluck the pillow from his hands and stuff it behind me. "Nah, this is fine for me. Won't be my first time crashing on a couch. But . . ."

"I'll handle him," Benji signs, already knowing what I'm worried about. "He's not concerned about you cheating with his mute brother, don't worry."

I hate that he feels that way, but my shoulders relax a little. Jessie isn't a bad guy, but he's got a temper at times. Especially where other men are concerned. He says it's just because he loves me so much and he's afraid he'll lose me. That's sweet . . . so why doesn't it feel sweet?

"I'll let you get some sleep," Benji signs as he goes to stand.

"Wait!" I grab his arm. "If you aren't tired, you could watch this show, yeah? I could use some company."

It's the truth. I don't know this place, and I'm feeling a little uneasy. The only thing familiar is Benji, and despite his rough exterior, he feels like a safe space right now.

He settles on the other end of the couch, and we watch the show. The comedian makes a good joke and I laugh, but when I look over at Benji, he's stone-faced.

Awkward.

"Not funny?" I ask. "Your brother doesn't find things funny either."

He shrugs. "I've seen this one before."

Minutes later, another joke comes out of the guy's

mouth, and I almost hold back my laughter for fear of embarrassing myself. Jessie hates when I laugh too loud at stupid things. But I let it out anyway. To my surprise, Benji lets out a silent laugh too, his lips drawing away to showcase his smile.

Benji looks at me. "Okay, that one gets me every time."

"I'm glad to have someone to laugh with me," I sign back.

Benji's smile softens as he watches my hands. "Do you really have a deaf brother?" he asks.

"Yes, he's in college now," I sign.

A smile crosses his face when I sign back at him again.

"I like that you speak my language," he signs, a sinful smirk following it. Then he hesitates. "Can I ask you something?"

I nod.

"Why him?"

"Who?"

"My brother."

My mouth gapes. How does someone even answer that? Jessie has been great to me. Mostly. He has a little bit of a temper, but no one is perfect. This line of questioning is making me a little uneasy, if I'm being honest.

"Jessie treats me fine," I sign.

"Fine? Not good? Not great?"

This conversation has taken a really uncomfortable turn. I'm about to stand up and leave when Benji's phone vibrates on the table. We both look down and see an incoming text from Jessie.

Benji snatches up the phone and starts typing.

"Oh shit. He's pissed, isn't he?" I ask, the uncomfortable convo forgotten for now. "I knew this was a bad idea."

Benji shakes his head and shoves the phone toward my

face. I read the message, which is just Jessie thanking his brother for babysitting me for the night. Benji was right. He's not pissed at all. He almost seems relieved.

"I told you he'd be okay with it," Benji signs after lowering the phone, but he doesn't hit play on the comedy show. "I'm sorry for asking you all that."

"It's okay. I just . . . Jessie's not a bad guy." Why am I defending him to his brother? "I think I need to get some sleep now."

Benji nods and goes to stand. He stops in the doorway and turns back. "Will you promise me something?"

"That all depends," I sign back. "If you want me to promise I'll leave my panties behind, it's a no."

That gets a silent laugh out of him. "No, just . . ." His hands hang in the air. "Promise me that if he ever stops treating you well, if he ever hurts you, you'll leave."

"Jessie wouldn't."

"Then it should be an easy promise to keep."

I tighten my lips and force out a nod, even though I know it won't happen. "I promise."

Benji nods once, then shuts off the light and leaves me to sleep.

CHAPTER SIX

BENJI

The next morning, I'm up bright and early so that I can make a pot of coffee for Emmy before ferrying her back to my brother's clutches. I wish I could make her something more substantial, like eggs and toast, but Jessie hasn't given me money for groceries this week. Maybe Emmy was right. I should get out more. If I didn't depend so fully on Jessie, maybe I could get out from under him a bit.

She's snoring lightly on the couch as I start the pot brewing something dark and fragrant. Her eyes flutter open as the aroma drifts toward the living room. She sits up and blinks at me after rubbing her eyes.

"Morning, stranger," she signs.

"Morning," I sign back with a smile. "Sugar and milk?"

"Milk, yes. Sugar, no. It's too early for sweet stuff."

I prep her mug and carry it to her. She takes a sip and closes her eyes, reveling in the warm beverage. She sets it on the table with a sigh, then stands and stretches. I have to tear my gaze away from the perfect arch in her back as her black t-shirt rises.

"Are you taking me to Jessie's, or should I catch a bus?" she asks. "It's daytime, so a bus is probably fine. I don't want to put you out."

"You aren't putting me out. I'll take you back."

She gathers her things, and we head to my car. After a short drive, we pull up in front of Jessie's house again. The sprinklers to the right of the driveway have just come on, so I park in the street so that Emmy isn't doused the moment she exits the car. Now she can walk up the left side of the path and stay dry.

Noticing, she smiles at me. "Hey, thanks for that. Your brother usually just parks in the driveway and screams something about a wet t-shirt contest as I scramble into the house." She offers a small laugh, but the smile is even smaller. "Anyway, thanks for this."

I follow her up the walkway. Jessie greets us at the door, already dressed in a button-up and khakis at this early hour. He kisses Emmy's forehead before ushering her inside, saying something about how her little gray shit stain has been driving him crazy. He closes the door behind her as she enters, remaining outside with me. I bristle, anticipating what's to come. Better me than Emmy, though.

"Hey, thanks for last night." He glances behind him to be sure the door is shut. "You really covered down. Wasn't necessary, but I appreciate you looking out."

My eyebrows pull together. "What are you talking about?"

"Don't play dumb now," he says with a punch to my shoulder. "That chick last night? She totally wanted me. You took Emmy back to your place so that I could get some strange without pissing off the old lady. I knew I could count on you when it really mattered."

That's not why I took Emmy back to my place, but I'm not about to tell him that. This is the out she needs, because if he learns that she forgot the precious fucking house key last night, there will be hell to pay.

I also can't tell Emmy the truth. If she learns that Jessie tried to cheat on her last night, she'll want to confront him. That has never ended well in the past. The last woman who called him on his bullshit ended up in the emergency room with three broken bones and a missing tooth. I encouraged her to call the police, but he paid her off. He always pays them off. That's how he keeps getting away with this shit.

No one listens to me when I try to warn them. That's the most frustrating part. Hell, what little warning I offered Emmy almost backfired last night. No, I can't tell her. I'll have to find another way to get her away from him.

"It's too bad it didn't work out," he says with a shake of his head. "Can't win them all, though."

"So you didn't cheat on Emmy?" I sign.

Jessie rolls his eyes and looks behind him again. "No, I didn't cheat on Emmy. I'm losing my edge."

"Why even date these girls? Why ruin their lives?" I sign, but he just turns around and opens the door. It's easy to ignore my valid points when I can't speak them aloud.

"Did you want to come in for a bit, or do you need to get going?" He doesn't turn around to see my reply. Another common tactic for Jessie. He just makes up my reply in his head. "Yeah, I guess after keeping up with my little hellion for the night, you're probably tired, huh?"

He goes to close the door, but I stop it with my hand.

"Any chance you could give me some cash for food?

The cupboards are a bit bare," I sign once he's finally looking at me.

He clears his throat and drops his voice to a whisper. "And you'll keep this savior shit to a minimum?"

"I'm not trying to be a savior. I just don't like the way you—"

He swats my hands. "Stop, dude. She might see you." He reaches into his pocket and fishes out a few twenties. "Here, take this until I can get by the bank."

He closes the door in my face. Yeah, maybe it's time I stop depending so much on my brother.

I get a disability check each month, but Jessie convinced me to let him handle it. Saves me from having to deal with the hassle that is communicating with people who can't understand me. That's what he said, anyway. I later realized it was just a way to keep me under his thumb, and honestly, I didn't give a shit.

Until I did.

Until his problems became my problems.

I can't watch him hurt Emmy.

There has to be some way I can help her without causing further harm. That's all I can think as I sink into the driver's seat and start my car. If I tell her the truth about him, she'll just run back to him and end up in a bigger mess. I've seen it before. I know how it goes. It's a cycle that doesn't break until bones do, and sometimes . . . not even then.

I pull out of the driveway and head toward home. There isn't an easy solution to the Emmy problem, but I think I know how to get myself out from under Jessie's complete control. It starts with a job, and I know right where I'll apply first.

CHAPTER SEVEN

BENJI

The parking lot is pretty empty when I pull up to the restaurant. It's been two weeks since I applied, and the manager just got back to me. There was no interview, no meet-and-greet to see if I'm a good fit. He just sent a text that said to be here at two, so here I am.

I swipe my hands on the black slacks and try to steady my nerves. While I'm used to wearing black, I'm not as accustomed to wearing dress pants. How does Jessie deal with the nut-crushing crotch? I can't wait to get back into denim.

Soft rock music drifts from the speakers, and the scent of fried food wraps me in a hug as I step through the doors. My eyes take a moment to adjust to the dim lighting as a large man comes toward me and holds out his hand.

"You must be Benji Rinehart," he says as soon as I walk in. "I'm the manager. Name's Dale."

I accept the handshake and give him a nod.

"You didn't list much work experience. You're not a slacker, are you?"

I shake my head.

"Hmm. You don't talk much either."

"I don't speak. Is that a problem?" I sign. "I mentioned it on my application."

The application he clearly didn't bother reading. His eyebrows pull together, and he glances around for help.

Emmy rounds the corner, and I don't think her eyes can go any wider when she spots me standing here. "Benji?" she gasps. "What are you doing here?"

"You two know each other?" the manager asks.

Emmy and I shrug. "Sort of," she says.

"You know sign language, don't you?" he asks. "Can you train the deaf guy?"

Emmy rolls her eyes. "He's not deaf."

Her manager's cheeks flame red. "You're off hosting and on training duty, then."

"What? No. Can't—"

"No, Emmy. You're training him."

He wanders off, denying any chance for her to argue. But why is she arguing? Is training me *that* bad?

"I see why you don't like him," I sign. "Sorry to ruin your shift."

She sighs and covers her face with her hands. "Sorry, Benji. It's not you." Her hands fall away, and she stares at me. "Wait, why are you here? Did Jessie send you to babysit me some more?"

I shake my head. "No, he doesn't even know."

Her shoulders relax a bit.

"I haven't seen you with him the last few times he stopped by my place," I sign. "Are you two still a thing?"

I hold my breath and wait for her response, hoping she

says they've broken up. He hasn't mentioned the incredible sex in days, so they've either split or he's getting bored. The second option is far more dangerous for Emmy.

"Is that what this is?" she signs back, her shoulders tensing again. "You're just here to see if I've kept my promise after your warning?"

I won't admit that she's partially correct. It's no accident that I've gotten a job here. She's still in the honeymoon phase with my brother, but I know what's waiting in her near future. I've seen the bruises. The marks. I've watched the tears. Yeah, part of me wants to keep an eye on her.

But I can see that this isn't going how I thought it would. I need to think of a new way to approach this.

"Can we start over?" I sign. "Hi, I'm Benji." I hold out my hand, and she finally relaxes.

"Hi, I'm Emmy, and I guess I'll be training you," she signs back with a guarded smile. "Just . . . no talking about Jessie, okay?"

I give her a salute as my heart sinks to my ass. If she's wanting to keep Jessie off-limits, that means she's hiding something.

As she leads me to the supply closet to show me where they keep the cleaning shit, I study her gait, watching for any limping or favoring of any part of her body. Each time she turns to say something, I study her face for caked-on makeup to cover a bruise. The lighting is either shit or she's in the clear. I'm okay with the second option.

When we go to exit the supply closet, we bump right into the manager. He side-eyes us, and Emmy's cheeks flush a shade of guilt-laden red. Nothing happened. She doesn't need to look or feel guilty.

"What are you guys doing in there?" Dale asks.

Emmy starts stammering, and it only makes us look

more guilty. I raise the bottle of cleaner and give it a shake. That draws Dale's attention to me, and the moment he remembers my disability, he turns tail and walks the other way. My inability to speak is a gift at times, especially when it makes someone that uncomfortable.

Not Emmy, though. She presses her hand to her chin and extends it to thank me.

I smirk. "Don't thank me. Just get better at thinking on your feet."

She throws me a salute before we head to a table with a cloth and a spray bottle, where I show her that I am absolutely capable of washing a table on my own.

"You hardly need me," she says with a smile.

"My voice doesn't work, but my hands always get the job done," I sign, followed by a wink that I regret. The unintentional sexual innuendo doesn't hit me until afterward. Thankfully, Emmy doesn't take it the wrong way, and she just gives me a polite laugh.

A trendy pop song comes on, and I nod my head to the tune. It's weird for a guy in all black to groove to pop music, I know, but we all have guilty pleasures, and mine happens to be pop music. If anyone else asks, I only listen to hard rock and screamo.

"I love Katy Perry," Emmy signs as I straighten the condiment caddy and move to the next table. "Well, prespace-exploration Katy."

I lower the rag to the table to give me use of my hands. "How do you and my brother get along, then? He hates pop music."

"Oh . . . I just don't listen when he's around."

"Sorry. I forgot the no-Jessie rule."

She sighs and grabs a rag to wipe the booth seat. "No,

it's fine. He's my boyfriend *and* your brother, so he's bound to come up. It was a stupid request."

I gently touch her arm to get her to look at me. "It wasn't stupid. I knew what you meant, and I'll keep my nose out of your business. Just know that if you ever need to talk?" I raise my eyebrows.

She gives me a genuine smile this time. "Thanks," she signs.

I release a sigh of relief. Maybe this won't be so bad after all.

Or maybe I'm just a man who's desperate for his brother's girlfriend.

The urge to keep my brother's love interest safe has never clawed at me so fiercely. Normally it's just a nagging conscience, but this goes so much deeper. Normally the fantasy ends with the girl getting away safely. Now I have visions of what it would be like to rebuild the world my brother has demolished. To take each brick he's pulled from her and slide it back into place. I've only witnessed the destruction before this, but now? Now I want to witness the rebirth.

For the time being, however, I just need to focus on keeping her safe. Any fantasy I have of a life with Emmy is just that. A fantasy. She deserves so much better than my brother.

But she deserves so much better than me, too.

"Haven't seen you around much," she says. We move to the next table before she continues. "You and your brother don't hang out much, I take it?"

We actually used to hang out quite a bit, but I have a feeling he's been trying to keep Emmy away from me and my savior complex, as he calls it. I just call it having a sliver of a fucking conscience, which isn't the worst thing to have.

I can't tell her this, so I just shrug.

"He said something about watching the fight tonight. Maybe you should come too?"

My gut clenches. If Jessie plans to watch the fight, then Jessie plans to do some fighting himself. His little nose habit and a televised fight almost always go hand in hand.

"Yeah, I might swing by," I sign.

"I'd like that," she says. "Your brother probably would too."

No, he definitely wouldn't, but maybe he doesn't have to know I'm there . . .

CHAPTER EIGHT

EMMY

By the time the Uber drops me off, I'm too exhausted to do much more than drop onto the couch and ease the shoes from my aching feet, so I trudge toward the front door with plans to do exactly that. I ended up working longer so that I could train Benji on more than just bussing tables and wiping shit down. Dale doesn't think he should be around customers, but I beg to differ. He communicates just fine, voice or no voice. That's a fight for another day, though. Right now, I just want to rest before I wash the sweat off my body.

The lights are dim when I enter, so I assume Jessie's still at work. He works late some days, which is fine by me. It gives me a moment to breathe and play with Lily.

"Where is my little lady?" I call as I stroll down the hall.

Hearing my voice, she mewls back, but she doesn't come running to greet me like she usually does. I follow her desperate cries to the hall bathroom, where she's been shut inside in the dark.

"Oh, honey," I say as I bundle her into my arms. "Mommy is so sorry. I must not have noticed you in here before I left for work. You're probably so hungry."

At the mention of food, she leaps from my arms and starts down the long hallway, looking back at me every few steps to make sure I'm following.

"Yes, I'm right behind you," I say with a smile.

As we pass the front door, I hear a car door shut outside. That sound used to make me excited, but for the past few days, I've had the opposite reaction. Invisible eggshells appear at my feet, and I'm on high alert for anything that might set him off. I spot a mug on the counter and hurry to get it into the sink before he sees it. Never mind that he left it there this morning. It's my job to tidy up. It's the least I can do since he doesn't ask me to split the rent or anything.

Jessie has never said as much, but that's the way I feel about it. Any sort of clutter sends him over the edge, regardless of who made the mess, so I just try to keep things clean so that he has one less thing to stress about. He's under a lot of pressure with work.

The door swings open just as I'm rinsing the mug. Crisis averted. I swing around and offer a smile as he enters the kitchen.

"Hey," I say. "Another long day at the office?"

He tosses some envelopes onto the counter and looks at me like I've offended him. "What's that supposed to mean?"

"Oh, I didn't mean anything by it. Just making conversation." I shrug and wipe my hands on a tea towel. "You'll never guess who started working at the restaurant today."

"No, and I doubt I'll care, either. All the people you work with are small and insignificant. You don't belong there."

"Jessie . . . could we maybe table the job discussion for now?"

He leans against the counter with a smirk. "There is no discussion. I want you to quit working there. Now it's up to you to do your part. You don't need to work, baby. That's what you have me for."

He pulls me into him and places a kiss on my forehead. I just stand here and let it happen. Arguing is pointless. He can't make me quit my job, though. Not happening, and for a very good reason that he can't find out about.

"Did you still want me to order wings for the fight?" I ask as he pulls away.

"You haven't done that already? Fuck! The fight's in two hours!" He checks his watch and pulls away from me. "I guess that's getting heaped on me too? Damn, you're just full of fuckups today, huh?"

"I didn't fuck anything up. Why do you constantly put me—"

His hand wraps around my arm so tightly that it sucks the air from my lungs. With a sharp jerk, he snatches me around to face him. "I told you to order the wings as soon as you left work so that you could pick them up on your way home. Now I'm already home, and they haven't been ordered. Now I have to leave again. Or is that what you wanted so that you could text *Dale* some more? Did you think I wouldn't figure it out?"

"What? Jessie, no! I—"

"Unless your next sentence is that you love me and would never, I suggest you shut the fuck up, yeah?"

"I do love you," I whisper. "He's my manager. We don't talk unless it has to do with work. You're hurting me."

I try to get my arm out of his grasp, but he only tightens his hold.

"Let's play a little game. I'll take your phone with me, and if Dale doesn't text you the entire time I'm gone, I'll believe you. Deal?"

I fight the urge to roll my eyes as I shove my phone into his hands. "If that's what you need, fine. Dale has no reason to text me. I already have my shift assignment for the week, and . . ."

My voice trails off as I remember our new employee. There is a very real chance that Dale might text me to let me know what Benji needs to work on. It doesn't matter that the content will be completely innocent. Jessie will find a way to spin it.

I pull the phone back. "Wait, he might text me about our new employee."

"Is that a code for something?" he asks. "Tell me the truth, Emmy. Don't lie to me."

I'm not lying, so why does it feel like I am? How does he have the power to make me feel like I've done something wrong when I know I haven't? My body responds with signs of guilt—flushed cheeks, sweat, rapid heart rate. Benji's warning whispers in the back of my mind.

"I can't do this," I whisper. "I love you, Jessie, but you can't treat me this way."

My body braces for impact. Jessie has never hit me, but Benji's secretive warnings raise their voices in my mind. They're shouting. If he's going to strike me, now would be the moment.

But he doesn't. He takes a step back and rubs his eyes. "Oh, fuck, what am I doing?" he whispers. "I fuck things up every single time."

"Are you . . . crying?" I ask.

He sniffles and wipes his eyes as he turns away from me.

"What do you care? Just get your stuff and go. I don't want my issues mucking up your life."

"You aren't mucking anything up, but I can't live under this constant scrutiny. I'm not a cheater, yet you treat me like one."

"All of my exes cheated on me. I can't help feeling like it's going to happen again. I'm just so scared of losing you. You're the only good thing I have in my life." He motions around to his house. "This place? My cars? My career? They're all just things. You give my life meaning. Without you . . ." He shakes his head and grips the counter. "Just go."

Is he seriously threatening to hurt himself? I can't have that shit on my conscience. I step closer and place a hand on his back.

"Hey, I'm sorry. I know you've been through a lot in your past relationships. Maybe we can find a way to work through this, huh?"

He turns around and pulls me into him. As he brushes his hands over my back, his touch is gentle, unlike the way he just manhandled me. "No, I'm the one who's sorry. I had a bad day at work, and instead of talking to you about it, I blew up on you. I'll work on it, okay?"

I nod up at him. "Okay."

"Besides," he says with a laugh, "it's not like you'd really take off and leave. Where would you even go? You don't have a car, and your apartment is probably long gone. You're stuck with me, Emmy Lewis."

He holds me against him and kisses the top of my head, but his words provide little comfort. If anything, I'm realizing that I might be in a mess after all.

"I'll go get those wings. You put on something cute so you can distract me between rounds." He smacks my butt and earns a nervous giggle. "I love you."

"I love you too," I say, but I'm not so sure I mean it anymore.

CHAPTER NINE

BENJI

I saw the finger-shaped bruises on Emmy's arm last week. It was the night after the fight she invited me to. I saw the way she looked like the entire world weighed down her shoulders too. Even though I noticed, I didn't mention it to her. There weren't any marks on her face, and her eyes weren't puffy from crying. I could only hope that whatever happened, it was enough to open her gorgeous eyes so that she realizes the danger she's in.

Every day since, I've kicked myself for not showing up that night. If I had been there, I could have stopped him or taken the brunt of his anger. Instead, Emmy was forced to bear that burden alone. There's another televised fight tonight, and it should be starting within the next thirty minutes. She invited me over again, but I declined.

I have plans.

I have to find a way to protect her from him before it happens again. He usually has a cooldown period after a blowup. That's when he flashes cash and showers them with affection and sweet words. This is usually when he moves them in too, but he jumped the gun on that one. Not that I blame him. We both recognize what a catch this girl is. It's just too bad she chose the wrong brother.

But back to that cooldown period . . .

It can't last much longer. The hits will start coming harder and faster, and if Emmy doesn't step out of the ring, she's liable to end up crumpled on the mat. The thought alone sends a spire of rage through my insides. I can't let him do worse than he's already done.

I pull my car behind a small gas station, put it in park, and step out. The camera gets a smile and wave from me as I stride out of frame and head down the street. I light a cigarette as I walk. I'm already out of place as I approach rows of McMansions on the expensive side of town, and my nerves are taut. The nicotine helps smooth things out in my head.

It probably doesn't help my case that I'm in black-on-black after dark, but it is what the fuck it is.

After looking around to make sure no one is watching, I slip up the driveway of a house that's set back from the road a bit. I slide past the garden fountain and slink into a mass of shrubbery. Thorns gouge my legs through the black denim, but I'm too focused on the window in front of me to give a shit.

Fingerprints smudge my view, but it's the best chance to get a glimpse of her behind my brother's hellish gates. Does it suck that it's also above the densest rose bush ever created? Yes, but I have to make sure the only violence in that house is on the television.

Inside, everything appears quiet. Emmy sits on a long brown couch in front of a large flatscreen. Her kitten swats a bit of paper on the floor. My brother appears from around a corner. He's swiping his nose an awful lot, so I can only assume what he just went to the bathroom to do. He flops down on the couch beside Emmy and wraps his arm around her. As she snuggles against him, my insides flame hot.

I often wonder . . . if I had a voice, would things have been different for me? Could I have been a smooth talker if I could talk at all? Could I have been confident like him? Maybe then I would have had a chance with someone like Emmy *before* she became involved with someone like Jessie.

It probably doesn't help that I've made sure I look like the least approachable person in town. The piercings. The fuck-off tattoos on my fingers. The mostly black attire. Yeah, I don't know. Maybe a voice wouldn't help matters.

On the television, two men throw hands and batter each other on the mat. Blood sprays. Jessie cheers. Emmy looks disinterested. I don't blame her. The fights never interested me, either. I'm starting to feel a little foolish for standing out here. Maybe I was wrong about my brother. Maybe he's changing.

If there were ever a woman to do it for, it's her.

The fight goes to a break, and Emmy's phone lights up in the darkness. Jessie reaches forward to grab it before she can. He's already primed to fight. Whatever he just saw on her phone has woken his evil spirit. My hands clench into fists at my sides, and breath saws in and out of me.

He stands to his full height, yelling and pointing at the phone. I can't hear him, and I'm no good at lip reading, but I can see the giant vein bulging at his temple. I can almost smell the alcohol on his breath. He tosses her phone onto the table and folds his arms over his chest.

I glance at Emmy. He has her penned up. His hulking frame stands between her and the only exit out of that room. She cowers on the couch, flinching with each syllable he enunciates with a shout. This is nothing like the strong girl I see at work. This isn't the woman I've watched toss out a table of drunks for pinching her ass. Jessie has done what Jessie has always done and wrenched any spirit from her body.

But then she finds her spark. She sits a little straighter and raises her chin as she shouts something back at him. The kitten skitters under the couch as her feisty owner yells at the brute. I'm equal parts proud and terrified. Terror takes first place as he charges closer to her, though.

With a snarl, he fists her hair and drags her off the couch. I don't need to be a fly on the wall to know what he's saying.

"Don't you ever talk back to me."

"Who the fuck do you think you are?"

"I could fucking kill you."

Take your fucking pick. I can guarantee it was one of them.

And I can guarantee I can't watch another second of this.

If Emmy can't find the strength to protect herself, then I'll be strong for her until she can. I glance around the garden, and my gaze lands on the large decorative stones lining the path. I tear myself away from the window and sink my fingers beneath one of the stones. Grit and cold earth bar my way, but I push past until I free the rock. My fingertips are cut and bleeding by the time I pull it from the soil, but it's nothing compared to whatever he might do to her. With a grunt, I raise the stone and shuffle back to the window.

She managed to escape his grasp. She cowers in the corner, terrified and shaking as he stalks closer. As I raise the rock, I can't help but wonder if it will be enough. Will she leave him after this? Will she finally find the strength to walk away?

None of that matters, though. No matter what she does after this, I have to try.

Before he reaches her, I send the rock into the window. Glass shatters, and their startled screams reach me through the large hole. They cover their heads and move away, but their shock won't last. I can't stick around to see how this plays out. Jessie will want to beat the vandal's ass, and seeing how I'm the fucking vandal, I need to make tracks.

Without a second glance behind me, I race out of the garden and rush for the road. Why don't I feel better about this? I protected the girl. I saved the day. So why does my chest feel like someone hollowed it out and shoved sawdust into my veins?

Because it's not over.

I've protected Emmy this time, but what happens when I'm not there?

The sawdust crawls under my skin as I pick through backyards until I'm back at the gas station. This clawing, itchy feeling hasn't been a problem for years now, but I know just how to shove it back down. It's the same way I shoved it down for most of my life until one day I just stopped.

Stopped caring.

Stopped trying.

I just existed, pushing through one fucking day after another. I felt nothing, saw and heard and tasted less. I just . . . was.

And then she appeared, and I started seeing and hearing and tasting. I started trying. I started to care. That's what this horrible feeling is, and I have to make it stop. With the care comes the ache, the longing, the need for something

I just. Can't. Fucking. Have. For years, it was the desire for a normal life and a voice. Now?

It's her.

I race home to find the relief I need. My fingers practically itch to give me the release I crave, and my brain begs for the silence that will follow. When my mind goes quiet and the thoughts stop screaming, I'll be okay.

After slipping my car into a parking spot, I hurry into my apartment and head straight for the bathroom. Despite not doing this for years, I still have what I need in a drawer. I kept it, just in case I ever needed it again, never expecting Emmy to come waltzing into my life. What comes next *is* expected; she'll waltz right back out again. I just have to hope she's still intact when she does.

I pull the razor from its hiding place. Sweat coats my skin as salvation dances between my fingertips. The anticipation of a quiet mind for the first time in weeks is almost more than I can bear.

Raising my shirt and lowering my waistband, I find the scar just above my hip—one of many on my body, each one etched into my history as a constant reminder of the pain I endured and the escape I sought.

My fingertips go to my neck, to a dark mark inked there, and I'm reminded of the times I almost escaped. Permanently.

I sit on the toilet and tighten my grip on the shining blade. My teeth come together, and I place the sharp corner on the edge of the scar. When I drag the blade to the right, I don't rush it. No, I let the sharp ache linger. Stabbing pain rips through nerve endings and sends fire into my bones. Silence blankets my thoughts. I can only focus on that stinging fire and blood dripping onto the floor.

If it sounds romantic, I don't mean for it to. This isn't

anything I'm proud of. Hiding the scars is almost as important to me as hiding the reasons why I started cutting in the first place. My dirty little secrets.

I tip my head back and let the blood flow. When the pain starts to dull, I lean forward so that my waistband digs into the gash. I grit my teeth and gasp. It's wonderful.

This should keep those horrible thoughts of Emmy at bay. Whenever I think of her and all the ways I'd love to make her body mine, I'll just give myself a dose of pain to remind myself there are worse feelings than those of longing.

Yeah. There is always something worse. Whatever that means for Emmy, it isn't my job to care. I just don't know how to stop.

CHAPTER TEN

EMMY

Fear is a paralyzing emotion. I haven't experienced it often in my life. Maybe when I was a child and I thought the monster was about to drag me beneath the bed. The fear I'm coming down from now? I'd say it feels a lot like that. For the first time since meeting Jessie, I'm feeling truly scared.

I stare at a lone glass fragment sitting beneath the coffee table as he rants about how shitty this neighborhood is. He thinks some punk kid threw the rock through the window, but I think it was a guardian angel. I saw the way he was looking at me. If he hadn't been interrupted, I'd be dead or worse.

Standing against the wall, I try to make myself as small as possible as he walks around, assessing the damage. My hope is that he'll forget all about why he was pissed at me in the first place.

Shame and guilt rear their heads in my mind, which is bullshit. I did nothing wrong. Yet again, it was a simple text from Dale that set him off, and yet again, I'm left feeling like a cheating whore.

My phone buzzes again, and I snatch it up before Jessie has a chance to remember. But it isn't Dale this time. It's Benji. He wants to know if I work tomorrow so that we can ride in together. He doesn't like that I take the bus or waste money on the occasional Uber, but Jessie is too busy to ferry me all over town.

"Who's that?" he asks as he sifts through the glass and pulls up a large stone.

"What?"

"You're too hot to be so fucking stupid. You know what I asked."

He's called me stupid twice tonight. I'm not stupid. I'm not an Einstein by any means, but I'm not the idiot he makes me out to be.

"It's just your brother," I say. "He wanted to know if I work tomorrow. He's been taking me to work when we have the same shift."

I brace, fearing he'll accuse me of cheating with his brother now, but instead of getting angry again, his face brightens.

"Benji got a job? When did he start working there?"

"Not long ago. I've been training him."

He reaches for my phone, so I hand it over. He's fine when reading the messages between me and Benji, but when he flicks over to Dale's messages, his hackles rise. "Your boss sure texts you a lot. You trying to move up in your little job, Emmy? I bet he'd give you a raise if you got on your knees, huh?"

"He's not that kind of boss, but even if he were, I'm not that kind of girl. It hurts when you say stuff like that."

He rolls his eyes and tosses my phone onto the couch. I

let it lie there. If I go for it now, it might look suspicious, even though I'm not trying to hide a fucking thing. If he ever listened to me, he'd know how much I dislike my boss. He wouldn't be accusing me of anything sexual with that asshole.

When I moved in with Jessie, this isn't what I pictured. I didn't think I'd be wishing I still had the apartment to run home to. I never imagined I'd need safety. He was supposed to be my safe place. And he was. Until he wasn't.

Tears fill my eyes, and the adrenaline exits my body in a rush. I drop to the couch and put my face in my hands. I sob. This is the shit Lifetime warns you about. This is the shit we all say we'd never land in, yet I'm up to my fucking neck this time. I'm drowning in it.

"Why the fuck are you always crying?" Jessie shouts. "Jesus Christ with the waterworks. Shut the fuck up!"

The back of his hand collides with the side of my face, and I crumple to the couch. Shock silences me, and I lie here, frozen and waiting for whatever comes next. I'm too scared to move, so I just stay still.

Jessie's hand lands on my shoulder, and I fight the urge to recoil. "Baby, I'm sorry. I didn't mean to yell at you or hurt you. This is why it's so important for you to quit that job. It's just causing problems for us."

Words rush into my throat, ready for the argument. I want to say no, that my job isn't the problem here, but that will only cause things to escalate. The words slide back down to my gut, where they dissolve in a pit of shame.

"You might be right," I say instead, even though I don't mean it. Anything to keep the peace. "Maybe we should talk about it more when you aren't drunk, though."

He sits down beside me and pulls me into his lap. "Baby, I'm so sorry. I'll cut back on the drinking. You're absolutely right. You can't be the only one making sacrifices for this relationship. I'm willing to do whatever it takes."

His lips press against my forehead, and I force a smile. His kisses have never made me so uncomfortable before. It feels like allowing a cobra to brush its deadly fangs over my skin. Benji's warning resurfaces in my mind, and I don't know who else to turn to. I'll need to talk to him about this. Maybe he has some insight.

"I'm not really feeling the fight anymore," he says. He leans forward and clicks off the television, and my stomach sinks further. "Maybe we should go remind ourselves why we fell in love in the first place?"

His hand drops to my breast, and I want to disappear. I move his hand away and place it on my hip.

"Maybe we could just cuddle a little?" I place my hand on his thigh. "It doesn't always have to be sex."

His hand returns to my breast, and his mouth finds my neck. "But what if sex is what I want? Don't you want to make me happy?"

My eyes slide closed, and a tear slips down my cheek. I didn't even realize I was crying. "Of course I do," I whisper, and it's the truth. Even if it's for no other reason than I'm afraid of what happens when he's not happy. "But what about the window? Don't you need to get that patched over?"

He pulls back and looks me in the face. "Are you saying you don't want to have sex with me?"

"No!" I shake my head. "No, that's not it. I just don't want anyone to break in. That kid might come back."

He studies my eyes, but I've already fucked up. He knows this isn't what I want.

And he doesn't care.

"Then if you aren't saying no, it's a yes." There is no sly

smirk. No flirtatious wink. He isn't testing the waters. He's telling me.

And just like that, I let him walk me into the bedroom as if nothing happened. As if I want this when every cell in my body screams that this is wrong. I promise my body if it can just survive this a little longer, I'll get us out of here. We'll be safe.

What happens next feels like rape. I'm consenting, I'm participating, but I'm not doing any of it willingly. I'm a hostage in his home. The strong woman I thought I was has been replaced by a woman who is too afraid to say this isn't okay. My head drops to the side, and I cry silent tears as Lily bats a bottle cap across the carpet. I focus on her tiny, perfect paws until Jessie finishes inside me.

He doesn't offer to help me clean up. He just pats my ass and tells me to do it. I cry more in the bathroom, but it doesn't make me feel any better. Before heading back to bed, I check my face to be sure he can't tell that I've been silently sobbing. It's no use. The red rings around my eyes won't be tamed.

But it doesn't matter anyway. He's already asleep by the time I return. For the first time this evening, I take a full breath in and realize how truly fucked I am.

CHAPTER ELEVEN

BENJI

The second hand seems to move backward on the clock face as I push plates into the bus bin at work. Emmy is ten minutes late for her shift, and I'm starting to worry. I texted her last night, and she said she'd be in at lunch. Where is she?

"Excuse me?" a man says from a nearby table.

I try to keep walking as if I didn't hear him, but he reaches out and grabs my arm.

"Excuse me, can you tell me your specials today?" he asks. "My wife has a peanut allergy, so leave off anything with that in it." He offers a kind chuckle.

I want to answer him, but it's pointless. He'd just end up more irritated if I tried to communicate, so I shrug and hurry off. He scoffs behind me and will likely let Dale know I was rude to him. Wonderful.

I guess I should have expected that working in a restaurant would be difficult. Working anywhere is difficult when no one speaks your language. I tried college for a while, but even that was too anxiety inducing. Depending on Jessie worked for a long time, but how can I encourage Emmy to escape his clutches when I'm so dependent on him myself? If I can keep this job, I can make just enough to squeak by each month without needing Jessie's handouts. That's if I can convince Jessie to let me keep my supplemental disability check. Once I'm fully self-sufficient, I can really help Emmy get away.

The entrance swishes open, and my head jerks to the right so that I can see if it's her. It's not, and it's painfully obvious that I seek her out in every fucking person that walks in the front door. I couldn't be more embarrassing. It doesn't matter that she thinks she's in love with my brother. That she looks at him in ways she could never look at me. The sweet words she hands him.

Her moans.

I'd give my fucking life to hear her moan, even if those sounds can't be for me.

If I really wanted her for myself, I could take her. Whenever I fight my brother, I hold back. A lot. It wouldn't be difficult to use my hands to send a more memorable message than what ASL can accomplish.

Except for the fact that he's my *brother*.

That loyalty feels more like a chain around my neck at times like this. Or maybe it's always been a chain around my neck. How long have these familial ties cast blinders over my eyes?

I think back to when we were younger. I search for some memory of comfort or camaraderie, but my mind spits out moments of distance and indifference. Even when we'd get in trouble together, there was no commiseration in the bedroom as we wept over our tanned hides. If anything, I was in for a second beating because he needed somewhere for his rage to go, and a silent sibling seemed like a good enough punching bag.

It wasn't as if I could yell for help. No, someone else made sure of that.

A family stands and leaves a large mess behind, so I hurry over to the table to clean up. Maybe if I work a little harder, Dale won't say shit about me ignoring the old guy. The chemical smell wafts up as I spray the wooden tabletop in front of me. I lift the rag to start cleaning it, but I glimpse red hair from the corner of my eye. The rag falls from my hand, and I openly stare at Emmy walking past the hostess stand.

Something is different.

Something is wrong.

When she notices me watching her, she looks away and hurries to the back to clock in. I abandon the bus tub at the table. Fuck this job. I have to get to her and make sure she's okay.

By the time I get to the back, her apron is already around her waist and the smile on her face is practiced and perfect. She can't hide the bruise on her cheek, though. I see it like a neon sign beneath her makeup.

"Emmy, what happened?" I sign.

Her hand races to her cheek, embarrassment crossing her features. An ember of rage burns hot in my gut. She shouldn't be embarrassed. My brother is the one who should be looking like he's fucked up.

Because he absolutely has.

I've held on to some insane and desperate hope that he would adjust his ways for Emmy. That he would see a girl like her for what she's worth—*everything*. Her beauty and wit are enough to alter any man. She's certainly made a change in me. But Jessie having a change of heart? That was wishful thinking. He's still a venomous snake who hasn't shed his skin, and this time, he's menacing a woman I care about.

It's crazy that I'm so invested in her. I've spent so little one-on-one time with her, but there's something there that I can't explain. Some connection, like our hearts beat a little more in sync than we've admitted. An unseen tether binds me to her, pulling me toward her in a way I can't deny, even if it means my demise.

She makes me feel like I finally have a voice.

"What happened?" I sign again.

"I had a little too much to drink last night, and I slipped on the rug in the study." She shrugs. "Shit happens."

"Did he hurt you?"

"No, he didn't hurt me," she signs, though she won't look me in the eye. I guess she's too ashamed to speak the lie aloud.

I soften my features as much as I can. "It's okay to talk to me about it. You did nothing wrong."

She interrupts me with a flurry of signs. "I'm not as innocent as you think I am. This is my own mess, my own fault, and—"

I grab her hands and stop her from finishing the sentence. Absolutely not. Absolutely fucking not. I can't hold her hands and use my own, so I walk forward until her back hits the wall. I ease my hands off hers once I know she can't pull away from me. I tighten my lips because I feel the words wanting so badly to come from my throat.

"You've done nothing wrong. You're perfect. So goddamn perfect." I touch the right side of her face, and she winces. "No matter what imperfections he tries to leave on you, you need to remember who you were before him. And who you can be after him."

I care about Jessie because we came from the same division of cells, but I care about Emmy because she's the voice I've so desperately needed. She speaks to *me*, and I don't just mean sign language. She speaks a language known only to the two of us.

"You don't understand, Benji. I don't know how to get out of this now," she whispers.

She doesn't need to elaborate, and I don't have to ask her to explain. I understand so much more than she thinks I do.

I drop my hand from her cheek and dip it behind her neck. She doesn't flinch away from me as I pull her into me. I don't need to speak words for her to understand the intense longing I feel for her. The vibrations don't need to come from my throat. They already reside in every heartbeat thumping in time with hers.

I'm the worst brother on the planet. I shouldn't be in love with Jessie's girl, and I definitely shouldn't be kissing her.

But fuck it.

I close the gap and press my lips to hers. I give her time to pull away, to say this isn't what she wants, but she melts in my arms. She sighs and relaxes, and her eyes slide shut. Her hands go to my chest, but she doesn't push. She grips. She pulls.

She *wants*.

The kiss deepens, and I don't know who's doing it. It's happening to us, and we're just part of it. My hands drive through her hair, and she whimpers against my lips.

Then her eyes open, and like a bubble, the moment pops.

"Benji, I'm so sorry," she says before pushing out of my arms and hurrying away.

Yeah. I'm sorry too.

That was the worst thing I could have done. What was I thinking? She didn't need to be kissed. She needed me to listen to her, and instead, I did the same thing my brother does. I thought about what I wanted in that moment.

My fingers go to my lips. The way she kissed me kind of felt like she wanted it too, though.

And I don't know if that's better or worse.

WE FINISH our shift without talking much, which isn't typical for us. We usually take our breaks together, but every time I went for mine, Emmy was suspiciously busy. She's clearly avoiding me, and I don't know how to fix it.

I head to Jessie's house after I clock out. He's outside working on the window when I pull up. Emmy still has a few hours before she's off, and I wanted to get by here before she got home, so the timing is perfect; she lets me pick her up for work if Jessie isn't around, but she won't let me bring her to his place. She's paranoid about him throwing more accusations at her, but she hasn't learned our little safety net yet.

See, my brother's big flaw is that he doesn't believe his mute brother is capable of getting the girl. What he fails to realize is that I just haven't wanted the girls he's brought around. If I ever wanted to get laid, I went and got laid.

Pulling girls isn't the issue. It's always been the lack of desire to let someone in.

That all changed when Emmy walked up to our table. I finally saw someone who saw me. I just didn't speak up in time.

No fucking pun intended.

I get out of the car and walk toward Jessie. He hammers a board over the open window, and I feel zero urge to assist him when he reaches for the next one. I hope he gets a splinter, then transfers it to somewhere sensitive the next time he jacks off. It's the least he deserves for putting a mark on Emmy.

"Can you believe this shit?" he says. "We were watching the fight last night, and some punk kid busted out the window."

He's not actually asking if I believe it happened, because he doesn't even turn around to see my response. He just keeps nailing boards over the gaping hole.

"Repair guy can't get out for a few days, so I'm doing what I can until then. Emmy wouldn't shut the fuck up about her stupid flea bag getting out, so I stayed out of work to get it done."

How kind of him.

"Why didn't you tell me you needed more money? You didn't have to get a job at that dump."

"I did tell you," I sign behind him. He doesn't notice.

"Hey, hand me that hammer," he says.

I don't, which finally gets him to turn around. "You have to be nicer to Emmy," I sign.

His eyebrows pull together. "Maybe I need a crash course in ASL, because I know you aren't saying what I think you're saying. Benji, I've told you to stay out of my business when it comes to women. I know what I'm doing."

"I saw the bruise."

"And? She mouthed off! You remember when we were kids. If we mouthed off, we got popped. Well, not that you had to worry about that." He rolls his eyes and goes back to the window. "No, you were always nice and quiet, weren't you."

I grab his arm and force him to face me. "Emmy isn't your child. She's your girlfriend. And no one deserves to be hit."

"What did she tell you? That I fucking *hit* her? That lying bitch!" He throws the board to the ground and rams his hand into his pocket. "I can't believe this shit."

"She didn't tell me anything." I swat the phone out of his hands. "Listen to me!"

"You need your ass beat too?"

"She didn't tell me anything!"

He's finally paying attention now, so I keep going.

"I saw the bruise. I asked what happened, and she said she slipped and fell."

I regret saying this the moment my hands fall to my sides. This adds value to her in his eyes. A woman who will cover the bruise and its origin is worth keeping around forever.

"Then she's smarter than I gave her credit for." He laughs and plucks his phone from the grass. "Look, I already told her I'd lay off the alcohol. Happy?"

"It's not just the alcohol. Have you thought of getting help?"

"Not this shit again."

He turns his back to me, and that's the end of the discussion. It was a stupid discussion anyway. How could I have thought he'd change and treat her right? That will never be the solution. I see that now.

I hang around a little longer, listening to him have a conversation with himself, but this isn't going anywhere useful. I also want to be gone before Emmy pulls up and thinks I'm telling him about that kiss. I'm not dumb enough to do that.

And if she's a smart girl, a *good* girl, just like I think she is, she won't tell him either.

CHAPTER TWELVE

Emmy

My nerves are raw by the time I make the trek from the bus stop to Jessie's driveway. My fingertips keep drifting to my lips. Despite the way Jessie accuses me of it every fucking day, I've never been a cheater. Now I've done something unforgivable.

Because I kissed Benji back.

And because I want to do it again.

If this were any other scenario, I'd have broken up with Jessie the moment I realized we weren't right for each other. I'm not a clinger. I don't fight for something that isn't working, and I don't fucking cheat. Nothing is simple anymore. When he moved me into his place, that wasn't a kind gesture. It wasn't an act of love. It was about control, and in my blind love-haze, I fell for it. Now I'm trapped. Now I have nowhere to go and no one to turn to. It's not as simple as just going out and finding a new place for me. It's just not. I'm lucky I even have a job right now, and if Jessie ever learns about my dirty little secret, I'm really fucked. And I don't mean the secret about his brother kissing me.

Boards cover the broken window, so at least I can be grateful that he did as I asked and didn't let Lily escape. The house is quiet when I step inside, and I'm glad to see the counter devoid of any beer bottles today. I don't think I can handle another night like last night.

After I change into something that doesn't smell like fried food and barbecue sauce, I search the house for him. I round the corner and spot him sitting on the couch with his back to me.

"Jessie, we have to talk."

I swipe my hand over my neck to stop the hairs from standing on end as he turns his head and I witness his plastic smile. I've rehearsed this conversation in my head one million times, but I never pictured him smiling. That false joy nauseates me.

"What do we need to talk about, baby?" He tilts his head to the side. I once found that gesture so endearing. It reeks of condescension now.

I raise my chin to feign the confidence I so desperately need to show. "What you did last night wasn't okay. You can't hurt me like that anymore."

He shifts to look at me fully, and that's when I notice Lily sitting on his lap. He gently strokes her back as she squints happily at the ceiling fan. So why is my heart working at the pace of a hummingbird's?

Because you know what he's capable of . . .

My pulse finally slows as he lifts her from his lap and places her on the floor. He stands and circles the couch, coming to a stop in front of me. I fight the urge to flinch as his hands rise and cup my face.

"I know that, Emmy. What happened last night can't

happen again, and it won't." He bends and kisses the bruise on my cheek. "I'm sorry I did that. It's just . . . the thought of losing you makes me so crazy."

The sound of his voice makes me want to slink away from his touch. This isn't the sort of obsession I want from my partner.

I'll have to play nice for now, but that doesn't mean he can treat me any way he pleases.

"If you want this to work, then you have to stop acting like that." I take a deep breath and muster some courage for the next part. "Because I won't stay if you continue to hurt me."

I imagined his response to this so many different ways. Rage, contrition, hurt—these were the emotions I anticipated in every scenario. What I didn't anticipate was the joy I see. His eyebrows rise, and he laughs in my face.

"You'd leave me?" He shakes his head, his laughter rising. "Do you think you deserve better?"

Tears warm the backs of my eyes, but I refuse to let them fall. I raise my chin a little higher. "Yes."

His laughter dies to a scoff. "Interesting. And how does your employer feel about that little felony of yours? Does *he* think you deserve better?"

A cold tingle walks down my arms, and I can't feel my fingers. "I didn't—"

"Does September twelfth ring any bells?"

Yes, it does. It rings a lot of bells, but how the hell does he know that? It was a date that lives in my head because I've heard lawyers and judges bring it up numerous times. It was a day where I made a decision that I can't say I regret. I stole money to help someone I cared about, and I eventually got caught. It was something I never wanted Jessie to find out about, at first because I was embarrassed. Now it merely seals my fate and gives him one more thing to hold over my head.

"I made a mistake, and Dale knows about it," I say.

"I bet he does."

"What does that mean?"

Jessie shrugs and sucks his teeth. "You probably fucked him for that job, huh? You're probably still fucking him, even while you're with me."

"No, I've never cheated on you!"

I don't realize that's a lie until Benji's face flashes in my mind. My only hope is that Jessie doesn't see the guilt branded on my forehead.

He doesn't, but what he does next is still so much worse than what he's done before.

He grabs my hair in a tight fist and smiles down at me. "You can't leave me, baby. You have nowhere else to go. If I can't get Dale to fire you, I'll get his shit hole shut down. I'll follow you wherever you go, ensuring everyone knows what a lying snake you are. A thief. A fucking slut." He gives me a hard tug that sends sharp pains through my skull. I don't give him the satisfaction of a whimper. "And just so we are *crystal* fucking clear, no, you don't deserve better than me. You don't even deserve what I'm about to give you."

"Please don't," I say. It comes out of me before I can stop it.

He draws my head back and slams my forehead into the table. Sparkles and splotches appear before my eyes, and I stumble sideways.

"You're mine. The quicker you realize that, the better it will be for you. We can go back to how it was. I can spoil you again. You just need to stop being a stupid *bitch* who thinks she's better than what she really is. A petty thief. A dirty whore."

His flaming words land against my ear, but I'm still in a daze from the blow. My arms and legs move like they're being controlled by someone else. I barely register the sound of his zipper falling.

He rips down my sweatpants and pins me between him and the table as he cages me within his arms. He pushes inside me. Pain tears through me as he rams his hips upward. His grunts and groans twist my stomach as he rapes me.

He finishes inside me and leaves me panting and tearful against the wooden table. I reach back and pull up my pants.

He's right. I don't deserve this. I don't deserve any of it. Yet I endure it all.

And now that he knows my secret, it will never end.

CHAPTER THIRTEEN

Benji

Searing pain tears through my femur. I haven't injured the thick bone. No. The skin above it and all those delicate nerve endings scream out in agony. Blood fills the wound I carved into my upper thigh, and glorious silence follows. My brain can't process the emotional anguish and the physical destruction at the same time.

But it's so short-lived. My mind fills with thoughts of her, then with thoughts of filling her. More than that, I envision what it would be like to drag my tongue ring through her pussy until she pushes my head away and begs me to stop. It's vile and traitorous to imagine doing this to my brother's girlfriend, but I need to taste her more than I need my next breath. I've been torturing myself with these fantasies for hours.

Fuck, why isn't the cut doing its job? I need to stop thinking of her right now, but she's what my mind returns to. First she makes me reflect on my relationship with my brother, and now she's overpowering my unhealthiest coping mechanism. She's breaking me down and rearranging my psyche after one kiss.

Just a kiss.

Jessie is a fucking idiot. If she were mine, I wouldn't beat her if a man looked at her. It isn't her fault that her parents blessed her with incredible genetics. Besides, why take out my rage on the woman I care for when there's a perfectly good man to curb stomp into an early grave?

I've never considered myself a violent man, but for Emmy, I might change that. Unlike Jessie, I would do whatever I could to protect her if she were mine. Even now, I'll do what I can to keep her safe.

Anything but take out my brother.

I drive my thumb into the cut and open my mouth. Pressure builds in my head as I try to scream, but my throat is locked down. This pain goes deep enough to have me seeing stars, but not quite deep enough to dislodge the stone from my throat.

I slide to the floor and lean my head against the cabinet beneath the sink as I wait for the wave of nausea to pass. Blood gathers in a small puddle beneath my leg. The initial gush has slowed to a trickle. I don't cut deep enough to bleed myself dry. I cut deep enough to bleed out the memories and the emotional torment. But I can't be rid of it. That would mean bleeding out completely. These memories fester inside me, in my bones, in my soul. They won't stop until I take a final breath, and even then there is no guarantee. The echoes of my torment will follow me into that deep darkness. I'm almost sure of it.

My phone vibrates, and I pull it out of my pocket. It isn't Emmy, though. It's just Dale asking if I can cover for someone tomorrow. Of course I can. I'd live at that shitty restaurant if it meant getting more time with Emmy.

I lock my cell and shove it into my pocket as I rise from the floor. This sort of obsession isn't familiar to me. It's the sort of thing Jessie does with a girl, but I've never had the motivation. I never cared. My every waking moment is filled with schemes to get in her presence again. Because maybe if she gets to know me—the real me that no one else sees—I might convince her to switch sides.

As I pour a glass of water from the kitchen tap and gulp it down, I know that won't work. If I want Emmy to be happy, it means getting her away from my brother. There is no solution that ends with her in my arms. There just fucking isn't. I have to do what my brother can't. I have to make *her* the priority.

Ideas form and disintegrate while I mop up my mess from the bathroom floor. I wish it were so easy to wash away my trauma. No amount of scrubbing will ever make me feel clean again. Whenever I look in the mirror, I see the invisible marks his fingers made on my face and throat and—

My fist flies forward and shatters the mirror above the sink. Instead of shattering my face, I've multiplied. Thirty terrified little boys look back at me, and I don't know which one to apologize to first.

I exit the bathroom and flop onto the couch. That mirror was shit anyway.

It's getting late, but I'm not tired. I'm too worried about Emmy and what might be happening to her at this very moment. I lean forward and cut on the television to occupy my mind, but the comedy special Emmy watched pops into my recently watched feed. The entire universe is out to fucking get me.

I click off the TV and toss the remote back to the coffee table, but when I get to the bedroom, it's no better. As I lie back, I can't stop imagining what it would be like to have

her head on my chest. She'd be so small in my arms, so fragile. So *mine* to do with as I please. Unlike Jessie, I would
cherish her. Worship her. I would keep her safe and do
whatever it took to protect her. But my brother and I have
some similarities. I'd still want to use her body for my pleasure until she can't stand.

My dick hardens to the point of pain, and I grit my teeth
against the throbbing ache. As silly as it sounds, I don't want
to waste a drop of my pleasure. It belongs to her, and until
she brings it out of me, I don't want to come. In my desperate, obsessed mind, I'm saving it all for her, for that one
moment of weakness when she begs me to take her.

I may not be capable of killing my brother, but to deny
myself the knowledge of what Emmy sounds like when she
comes would kill *me*. When that moment happens, when
Emmy finally accepts that she wants me, I won't hold back.

CHAPTER FOURTEEN

EMMY

Shame tears a fresh hole in my gut as I get ready for work the next morning. Color correction works great for the greenish bruise on my cheek, but my neck is a different story. I've had to fasten a scarf around the dark marks, but they keep peeking from the top and bottom. There are too many finger-shaped bruises to cover.

Any hope of escape shattered the moment Jessie revealed that he knew about my secret. It doesn't matter that I stole the money to get my brother a car so that he could attend college. He received a scholarship for working hard in school, and with all the other challenges he'd been handed in life, I didn't want a lack of transportation to hold him back. I told our mom I worked overtime to earn enough, and she didn't question it, despite it being impossible to have worked that many hours. Once she learned what I'd done, she cast me out and said she'd raised me better. I've been struggling on my own ever since.

And while I would do it twenty times over to help my

brother, I wish things had been different. That they hadn't found out who stole the money. Maybe I could have a somewhat normal life.

Instead, a felony follows me around and makes me look untrustworthy. It took months to find a job that would accept me, and steady employment is part of my fucking program—a deferred sentence and fines so long as I keep my nose clean. If I lose this job, I'll have to go to prison. Dale wouldn't fire me because of my felony—I wasn't lying when I said he's aware—but if Jessie threatens him, I can't blame him if he lets me go.

Jessie enters the bedroom as I'm touching up my lipstick. He smiles and leans over me to place a kiss on my head. I close my eyes and let it happen.

"There's another fight this weekend. Want to get some wings and watch it together?" he asks.

"Sure," I say. My voice quivers, so I clear my throat. "Maybe we could invite your brother?"

"Why? Afraid to be alone with me now?" He runs his hands through my hair as we look at each other in the mirror. He hit the nail on the head, but I can't admit it.

"No, I just thought maybe he'd like to hang out. He keeps to himself at work and doesn't seem to have any friends."

His grip tightens in my hair, and water fills my eyes. "He's an idiot who can't speak. Who'd want to be friends with him?"

When I don't answer, he shakes me with his grasp on my hair.

"No one," I say.

"Exactly right, baby. It's fine to feel sorry for him. I fucking do." He dislodges his hand from my hair and adjusts the black scarf on my neck to hide the fingerprint bruises. "You know, it's summer and this looks *so* suspicious." He grips my chin. "Make it not suspicious, Emmy."

How did someone so sweet and giving become this monster beside me?

I'm not sure what happened or what caused it, but it's like a switch flipped inside him. Or maybe the caution lights have always been on, but I was too entranced by their brilliance to heed the warning. His brother tried to tell me, but I didn't listen. Now Jessie has something to hold over me, leaving me more trapped than I was before. So I reach up, adjust the scarf, and tuck the tail beneath my shirt.

"That's better," he says with a smile. "Everything will be just fine, so let's just forget we had to have this talk, okay?"

I nod and stare at myself in the mirror, but I don't recognize who I see anymore.

THE RESTAURANT IS DEAD TODAY, which is fine by me. The fewer people I have to interact with, the better. I'm a little sad that Benji isn't scheduled today. I think I'm finally ready to talk. Maybe.

Heat brushes my skin as I stride past the griddles and make my way to the back office. It's still dark back here, which means Dale hasn't come in for the day yet. I flick on the lights, grab my apron, and fasten it around my waist. After tucking my ticket book, pens, and some straws into the pockets, I hurry back toward the front.

I gasp as someone drags me into the supply closet. I've been here no longer than fifteen minutes, and something bad is already happening. Fighting against an immovable body, I panic in the darkness with a stranger's hand over my mouth. Did Jessie follow me here? Was it not enough to assault me at home?

The light clicks on, and I look up into Benji's face. Panic recedes, and I close my eyes and take a deep breath.

"Benji? What are you doing here?" I whisper. "You aren't scheduled to work today."

"I picked up a shift," he signs.

His lips draw into a frown as he looks at me. He rips down the scarf disguising my bruises, and what he sees darkens his eyes.

He tosses the scarf onto the concrete floor. "He's escalating."

"He made a mistake."

"Don't make excuses for him. You aren't stupid."

His accusatory glare and tone piss me off. I'm ready to talk, but I'm not ready to admit that I've royally screwed myself.

"I don't know what to do," I sign.

"Let me help you." He brushes the hair from my cheek, and that gentle gesture undoes me.

"Trying to seduce your brother's girlfriend doesn't seem like a very wise move," I sign.

He smiles and shakes his head. "I'm not trying to seduce you."

"Well . . . that's what you're doing, trying or not."

He smirks, and I can't stop staring at the black snake-bite piercings nestled beneath his full lower lip. He runs his tongue ring between his teeth, and my mind goes right back to that kiss. And it shouldn't. I shouldn't even know what kissing a tongue ring feels like. But I do. And I've thought about what it might feel like rolling over other places.

"I care about you," he signs, and his smirk falls. "In ways I shouldn't."

He leans closer, and now I'm inhaling each exhale of breath he creates. His fingers trace the bruises on my neck, and I don't miss the flinch of his lips as he tries to keep them from forming a snarl. By the soft tremble in his fingertips, I know he's trying to control his anger.

"Let me help you," he signs between us. "Let me deal with him."

I want to say yes, that he can confront his brother and save me from his clutches, but the thought of Benji getting hurt silences me. Because he isn't the only one who's developed feelings of care, and now I wonder how deep it goes.

On both sides.

Unable to say yes or no, I do the worst thing possible. I close the gap between us and kiss him again. His hands land on my hips and squeeze my black dress pants, urging me closer to him. His need presses against me, hard and sure. I want to reach between us and touch him, to let him know that I know, but I can't.

"Benji, I care about you too," I whisper into the kiss. "That's why we can't do this."

I expect him to nod and pull away, but he kisses me again, silencing my doubts. This isn't like Jessie, who takes what he wants. This is different. This is taking what I want to give.

He pulls away from the kiss. "Come to my place tonight when you get off work. We need to talk."

I nod, despite feeling like this is a very bad decision. I've either hit rock bottom and I'm on my way up, or I'm headed further down. Either way, I don't think things could get more complicated.

CHAPTER FIFTEEN

BENJI

Warm pain sizzles as I drag a razor over my upper thigh. Here recently, it's the only thing that dulls the inner ache. When I was younger, it was the desire for a life I'd never experience. Now? The woman I love is with my piece-of-shit brother.

It would be easier if I could just forget that an angel like her exists among us mere mortals. That's hard to do when I have to hang out with him sometimes. That means seeing them together or hearing about their exploits.

God, the thought of his body over hers tightens my gut until I feel like I might throw up. Then I imagine her moaning his name, and I dig the razor a little deeper. The pain isn't enough to overshadow my breaking heart, but I do feel the warm rush of blood. A lot of it.

I throw the stained blade onto the tabletop and drop both hands to my bare thigh. Yup, that's a bad one. This is what that girl fucking does to me. I'd spill every ounce of my blood if it meant I could have her. Even for a moment.

Blood spreads around my hand, and I pull off my shirt and hold pressure. I sure as shit won't go to the hospital with this wound. I can argue it was some freak accident all I want, but the ancient scars surrounding it would tell my truth.

There's a knock on the door. I completely ignore it, forgetting that I told Emmy to stop by after work.

"Benji?"

I wrap the shirt around my leg and pull up my sweatpants before heading to the door. She's halfway down the walkway by the time I get there, which is a bit of a problem when you have no voice. I will my inept vocal cords to do their one fucking job, and when they stubbornly refuse, I take a step outside and slam the door behind me. Emmy turns, and her green eyes flash at me like she wasn't expecting me to appear.

I put my hand to my forehead and wave it outward. "Hello."

God, I'm embarrassing.

She cocks her head at me, and I realize she's staring at my lap. I look down and see red staining the gray fabric.

"What the hell happened to you?" she asks as she rushes over and pretty much pushes me back inside my apartment. She touches her forehead and shakes her head. "You're bleeding."

"And you're bruised," I sign.

"Will you stop worrying about me? Pull down your pants."

I raise my hands to sign, but she grabs both of them.

"I know you're going to say something incredibly inappropriate." She levels me with a glare. "Don't."

She's not wrong, but I'm frozen. If I lower my pants, she'll see my scars. Which is something that never happened in my fantasies. I guess the scars don't exist in my mind, but they sure exist now. I pull my hands from hers.

"I'm fine."

"Don't be crazy," she says. "You're bleeding. Bad."

"Well, I'll take care of it. I'm not removing my pants."

Before I can stop her, she grabs the waistband and drops to her knees in front of me. Her fingertips work the shirt free, and my mind goes to terrible places as she looks absolutely horrified by what she's unwrapped.

"You need a hospital!" she shouts.

She goes to get up, and I grab her by her shoulder and hold her there. My mind goes to worse places, even as a warm line of blood runs down my thigh.

"No hospital."

"Why not?"

"I can't go back there. Not for this."

"Can't go back?" Realization washes over her face as she sees the scars etched down my thigh. "You did this to yourself?"

"Trauma is a messy bitch."

"Give me a minute," she says before handing me the shirt. She disappears into the depths of my apartment and returns with alcohol and Steri-Strips. She sits me down in a chair, pours alcohol on a rag, and gets to work cleaning me up. Any chance of not getting hard goes out the window when she looks up at me. Fuck.

"Why are you so good at this?" I sign.

"My brother used to get hurt a lot. He also didn't want to go back into the hospital. Albeit for other reasons."

She closes me up and looks around for something to wipe the blood off her hands. I lose all sense of control as I grab her left hand and bring it to my mouth. I lick the blood from her skin. Her mouth drops open, and my brain skids into dangerous territory. Fuck my brother at this moment. With her on her knees and her mouth hanging open like that, I have never wanted to put my dick somewhere more than I do right now.

Her hands rest on my bare thighs. They ease toward my boxers, and I don't stop her as she reveals my cock and the two black piercings lining each side of my shaft.

I pull her from her knees and draw her face toward mine. My forehead meets hers as I hold her there for a moment and think about how much I'll regret what I'm going to do next. I find that I won't regret it at all, but it *will* make me more feral for someone I can't have. I already eat, sleep, and breathe her. What would happen if I got to feel her around me? My mind won't know a moment of peace once I've experienced her.

I grip the back of her head and kiss her. I should feel bad about kissing Jessie's girl, but I don't. Not at all. Not even as I grab her hand and put it on my cock.

"We can't," she whispers against my mouth.

She's right, but that isn't stopping her from squeezing my length and stroking me until my toes curl.

"Darling," I sign, "I've never been so desperate for something. That's all I want to do to you. Let me make you feel good. Please."

The final desperate sign breaks her, and she nods at me. I stand and help her out of her pants. I wait for her to tell me no as I walk her backward until she's in the kitchen. When her ass hits the kitchen table, I grip her hips and lift her until she's sitting right at the edge.

"Have you ever felt a tongue ring on your clit?" I sign.

She shakes her head.

"Lean back, close your eyes, and find something to grab."

The moment her back lies on the wood, I'm on her. The moment the black barbell rolls over her flesh, she graces me with a beautiful sound. It's what I've fantasized and so much more. I wrap my hand around my cock as those euphoric sounds grow from every lash of my tongue on her clit. Her knuckles whiten with her efforts to grip the table's edge.

I pull away to look up at her and stroke myself to her pleasure. "I love the way you taste," I sign, releasing my cock just long enough to speak. "I want to drink from you. I want to *drown* in you. Darling, please come on my tongue."

My mouth lowers to her again, and I match the motions of my hand to the swipes of my tongue. I want to feel the same pleasure I'm giving her.

She releases the table, trading the wood for my hair. Her hands pull me deeper into her, and I pulse my hips into my fist as I devour her. Her toes curl as my tongue ring works her the way I know my brother never could.

"I'm going to come," she whimpers, and I push two fingers inside her. I want to feel her spasming around me. I want a taste of what my cock would feel if we weren't held back by obligations and familial ties.

She isn't the only one getting close, though, so I stop touching myself because it's too intense. She's the focus, not me.

But even without touching myself, those musical sounds stroke my shaft and pull the ecstasy out of me. While eating her pussy, as she comes on my fingers, I spill my load into my open palm.

When I'm certain I've lapped up every ounce of her pleasure, I stand and lean into her. I kiss her, and she lets me. But as soon as she comes down from her high, she pushes her hands against my chest and closes her eyes.

"We shouldn't have done that," she whispers, and the look of guilt all over her face hurts my heart. Why should she feel guilty for letting me make her feel good? Especially when all my brother does is hurt her.

I wipe my hand on my discarded shirt.

"We were just supposed to talk about how I can get away from your brother. This is so much worse." She covers her face and groans.

I pull them away so she can hear me. "Let me help you."

"And get you hurt in the process?"

I shake my head. "The only way I could get hurt is if *you* get hurt."

"This was a bad idea." She slides off the table and snatches her pants from the floor. "I don't know what I thought would come of this, but—"

She can't even finish the sentence, and I don't know what to say as she grabs her things and hurries out of the apartment. I thought the only thing I ever wanted was to get my voice back, but I think I've found something I want more. I'd remain voiceless forever if it meant I could have her.

CHAPTER SIXTEEN

Emmy

Jessie and I had three nice days. Mostly. Not great, but nice enough to make me question if he was serious about changing. And nice enough to make me feel guilty for what Benji and I did. He hasn't put a mark on me or even raised his voice. For the moment, I've nearly stopped walking on eggshells or feeling the unbelievable pulse of panic whenever my phone chimes.

Part of me hopes this is a turn for the better, but the other part of me is torn over his brother. Every moment Jessie is nice to me makes me feel like shit. And it shouldn't. His niceness doesn't negate the negativity or the fact that I have to find a way to escape him.

But for now, we're at the pier downtown, and I'm doing my best to play happy girlfriend at dinner with Jessie and his colleagues. They insisted he have a beer with them, so naturally, he's had at least six. My cheeks flush because I know what happens when he drinks.

The only other girl at the table looks as uncomfortable as I do. She's hardly said three words since we sat down, so I assume she's as trained as Jessie hopes I'll be one day. I tap her shoulder and gesture toward the bathroom. She nods and offers me a smile, and we squeeze from the table and head to the back of the restaurant.

"Thanks for saving me," the blonde girl says. "My name is Anna."

"Hey, it wasn't a totally sacrificial move," I say with a laugh. I don't think either of our boyfriends said more than five words to us tonight. Collectively. "Those boys sure can talk. I don't think I've said that much to a coworker in my entire time at my job. I'm Emmy."

She lets out a small laugh as we step into the restroom. She pulls lipstick from her purse, leaning over the counter to apply it in the mirror. "Jessie likes to command the room. I'm sure you know that, though."

Boy, do I. That presence is exactly how he got me in his grasp. He's sweet and playful in public—or when he's trying to get you to like him—but then he changes. I know who he really is. I'm surprised he's never shown that side of himself at work, even accidentally. Maybe he isn't like this with anyone but me.

"He doesn't usually bring his girlfriends around, so he must plan on keeping you," she says.

He might plan on keeping me, but I don't plan on being kept.

There's a knock on the door before I can even get to the stall. "Ladies, will you be joining us for dinner?" Jessie says through the panel of hardwood.

"We're coming!" Anna says. She turns back to me. "You finish up. I'll go keep them occupied."

I didn't really need to piss, but I go through the

motions and wash my hands before joining everyone at the table again. The waiter comes back for the tenth time to take our food order. Finally. I wait my turn to speak even though I'm already dreaming of the lasagna. It's the best here.

"Hi, yes," I say when it's my turn. "I'll have the—"

Jessie pushes my menu down. "She'll have the chicken Caesar salad and a red wine."

I open my mouth to correct him, but his hard eyes promise punishment. I swallow and sit back. His friends don't even seem to care that he just ordered for me. When Anna's boyfriend does the same and orders for her, she doesn't even look annoyed. She's also no longer looking at me at all. Great, now the only person who talked to me won't even give me the time of day.

The meal comes, and I finish my miserable salad in silence. Meanwhile, Jesse has moved on to liquor. He's on his second gin and tonic, and he's increasingly loud.

I stretch and fake a yawn. "Why don't we call it a night? I have to work in the morning."

There's a wave of agreement, and everyone pays up and gets ready to go. Walking to the car, Jessie's phone buzzes and he checks it. His lips twist and tighten, and my stomach twists in my gut. Whatever he just read pissed him off. He puts it back into his pocket, and his steps quicken. I can't keep up in my heels, and he's dragging me by the time we get to the car.

"What's wrong?" I ask, but he says nothing. I feel like I'm about to throw up all this rabbit food.

I get inside, and we drive back to his house. He remains silent, and I don't speak either. Whatever he's pissed about, I can't make it better, only worse. The drive drags on, and I feel like a child who's just brought home a bad report card.

The moment we walk in the front door, he starts yelling. "Did you think she wouldn't tell my coworker?"

"What?"

"Don't act stupid. You know what!" He scoffs. "Oh, wait. It's not an act. You're actually that fucking dumb."

I shake my head. I genuinely have no idea what he's talking about.

Red-hot pain strikes my cheek and sends me stumbling backward. Lily lets out a tiny yowl as my foot lands on a delicate paw, and she skitters away to hide. My hands fly up to baby my face. My mouth opens and closes as I fight back tears. I want to comfort my kitten, but that will only draw attention to her, so I stay where I am.

"Billy told me everything. You told his girlfriend I'm embarrassing because I have to be the center of attention."

I look up at him, shocked. All I did was agree with *her*!

"Jessie, I never said anything like that!"

"Bullshit! You made me look stupid in front of them. That's my boss, and now he thinks my own girlfriend thinks I'm embarrassing!"

His voice rises to an ear-splitting level, and spit flies from his lips and hits my chin. I would never have said anything like that because I know how Jessie would get if he felt mocked. I would never.

"Why would I say something like that when we've been having good—"

Another mind-altering strike slams into my face, but it's not a slap. This time, he used a fist. This time, it's my right eye. The force rocks me hard enough to send me to the ground.

"You fucking bitch! I tried to be nice to you! I fucking tried! And this is how you repay me?"

His fist hits me in the same spot a second time. I don't

feel bones crack, but I see a blur of red over my vision. My head swims as it feels like I'm drifting away from my body. A zipper falls, and I close my eyes and let darkness consume my brain. It's better there.

It's safer there.

And I let go.

CHAPTER SEVENTEEN

Benji

Emmy missed her last three shifts. She told Dale she's had the flu, but I know what probably happened. Jessie did what Jessie does. I tried to go by his place last night to get a glimpse of her through a window, but she never emerged from his bedroom. If she doesn't show up at work today, I'll break the fucking door down.

But she comes in around twelve, right on time. The thick makeup on her right eye hides fuck-all from me. He busted her open this time, and no amount of concealer can hide a gash.

Knowing she'll just try avoiding me again, I sneak up behind her and pull her into the supply room before anyone spots us. She does her best to keep her face turned away once I click the light on, but I've already seen it.

"What happened?" I sign. "And don't tell me you fell."

"He hit me. Happy?" she signs back. She turns to leave, but I grab her arm.

"No. Not happy. Furious." I brush her hair from her

cheek and study the bruise by her eye. "You're leaving him. Today."

"It's not that simple, Benji," she says. Tears fill her eyes as she keeps looking at the floor. Then she signs, "There are things about me that you don't know. I'm not who you think I am."

I step into her and take her into my arms because I can't stand another second of seeing her so dejected. "So, when I confront my brother later, will I be wearing you or not?"

"What?"

"When I tell him that you're leaving him, will it be with your come on my cock?"

"We can't," she whispers.

My hands fall lower, softly grazing her chest through her shirt. When I reach the hem, I give her a moment to say no, to tell me to stop. She should. But she doesn't. So I raise her shirt and drop my mouth to hers, inhaling her with a passion I've never known.

"They'll wonder where we are," she says as she eases her pants down her thighs.

"Let them."

I slip off my shoes and lower my pants just enough to free my dick. My hands drop to the backs of her thighs, and I raise her leg. Her warmth presses against my cock, and I close my eyes. She gasps as I push into her and the piercings rake her insides. Fuck, she's so tight. She lets out a whimper, so I throw my hand over her mouth. I can't speak without my hands, but I give her a shake of my head when she peers up at me. Her eyes roll in her head as I thrust deeper.

Words hang on my tongue, all those things I want to say and can't. She's beautiful. This feels incredible. The reality of her is better than any fantasy I could have conjured. I want to say all of these things, but my voice refuses to be heard. I can only hope she feels what I feel each time I push deep inside her.

She pulls my fingers into her mouth and sucks on me to keep herself quiet.

"Oh, good fucking girl," I mouth. Can she read my lips? I hope so. "Suck me, darling. Taste me."

My head tips back with the swirl of her tongue over each sensitive digit. Hard, yet somehow gentle. Soft, soundless groans leave my lips, and I'm lost to this pleasure. My mouth drops to her neck, and I kiss every bruised finger mark as I brace her back against the wall. Holding her like this, I grind against her clit and push deeper with each slow thrust.

Emmy's eyes widen, and her thighs begin to shake. I keep the same tempo, lulling her toward explosion with each grinding thrust. Her chest heaves, and her back arches, nearly ripping her from my grasp. I tighten my hold and fuck her through it until I'm certain she's spent. When I know she can be quiet, I pull my fingers from her mouth.

"Very good girl," I sign as I brace her against the wall.

She slides to her knees and reaches for my cock, clearly aiming to finish me off. I didn't want to get off inside her. I wanted this desire and frustration to remain inside me. To fuel me. I take a step back and shake my head as I pull up my pants.

"What about you?" she whispers.

"I told you," I sign. "I want your come all over me when I confront Jessie."

"You weren't serious about that, were you?" she signs, her eyes wide. "He'll kill you." She pauses. "And me."

"If it's my time to go." I shrug. "He's not putting his hands on you again. You could always stay at my place."

"No, that would really set him off." She looks down at

her feet. "I'm sorry I got you mixed up in this," she whispers.

I raise her chin and force her to look at me, and against my better judgment, I sign, "I'm right where I want to be."

I TOLD Dale I was sick and needed to leave early, but Emmy knows something is up. Her eyes are on me as I take off my apron and roll up my sleeves. I don't make it as far as the door before her hands rise.

"What are you doing?" she signs, and I fucking love that we're the only people in the room who speak this language.

"Don't worry about me, darling. Don't go home to him tonight, though. When you get off work, come to mine."

She shakes her head and tries to say something else, but I rush out the door. She'll either show up at my place tonight or she won't. I'm doing what needs to be done next whether she runs into my arms or his.

I get in my car and throw it in drive. My hands shake as I buckle the seat belt on my way out of the parking lot. I can't let that adrenaline wear off. The rush of blazing headlong toward my possible death has my blood running hot. But better my death than hers.

Jessie works from home a few days a week, so I know he'll be there when I arrive. I pull up the driveway and park. My hands are still shaking by the time I knock on the door. The moment the locks disengage, every muscle in my body tenses to the point of nausea. Not from fear, but from anticipation. When the door opens, I push him inside and slam the massive block of wood behind me.

"Benji, what are you doing here?" He chuckles and

peers behind me. "Go easy on the house, dude. What did it ever do to you?"

"I just came from work. I saw her face."

He has the audacity to throw his head back and laugh. "What excuse did she come up with for this one? She walked into a door? If she says anything to the contrary, I'll just say she's lying."

"And the finger bruises on her neck? How will she explain those?"

He puffs up to twice his size, but I don't back down. "You don't know anything about her, Benji, and you should really back the fuck off and remember where your loyalty should lie."

"With you, brother?" I shake my head. "I can't stand by someone who hurts a girl like her. Someone who hurts any girl, actually, and I've been silent for too long."

"Aw, did my baby brother finally make a friend?" He pouts at me. "She's only nice to you because you're related to me. Besides, staying silent is kind of your gimmick, isn't it?"

"I'm two minutes younger than you, asshole." I don't care about the other comments. They might have hurt a few weeks ago, but now his words are useless against me. I've been with Emmy, I've experienced my obsession, and now I'm ten feet tall and fucking bulletproof. "Let her go."

"You really aren't gonna drop this, huh? I didn't want to bring this up, but I guess you're forcing the matter." He sucks his teeth and looks past me. "Do you remember how you begged Mom to keep quiet about Mr. Ormsby?" He shakes his head slowly and finally meets my gaze. "Sure would be a shame if everyone learned of your very unfortunate and *very* dirty secret."

My legs move on their own, pistoning beneath me until

I slam into him. I throw my arm against his throat and pin him against the wall. My right arm rains down fists on his face, sending his cheek into the wall behind him. Blood splatters against the gray paint. I don't stop. I'm starting to think I might actually kill him after all, especially as those bruises pop into my head, but the shock wears off and he finds his feet. He throws his fist into my side, and I'm instantly winded. A silent scream tears out of me as the pain radiates through my back.

We drop to the floor and roll off each other, chests heaving. I have no threats to hold over him. Even if I ran to the police to bring up what he's doing to her, if she's unwilling to testify, they'll just sweep it under the rug.

"Are we finished here?" Jessie asks. He turns his head and spits blood onto the hardwood.

I sit up and try to take a deep breath, but my ribs scream at me. "We aren't finished until you're finished hurting Emmy. Either let her go or do better."

The motherfucker has the audacity to smile, revealing bloody teeth. "I'll try."

I hate him for that statement because it's not true. Yeah, he might *try* for a few days—maybe—and then he'll fall right back into his old patterns.

And I can't do a damn thing about it. Despite whatever I feel for Emmy, he's my brother. Short of murdering him, I don't know how to stop him. It also doesn't help that he's threatening to spill my darkest secret. I'm not ready to face my demons, and he's smiling in the face of his.

"She's staying at my place tonight. To give you a chance to cool down," I sign.

He groans and sits up, already ready for round two. "The fuck she is! Not that I'm worried about her shacking up with someone like you, but she's coming home tonight, and that's final."

"So much for trying, I guess."

Jessie grunts and gets to his feet. "Fine, fine. She can stay at your place tonight. See if I fucking care."

This isn't the end of it, but it's the end for right now. As he trudges deeper into the house, I make my exit. My point was made, and God help us all if I need to say it a little louder next time. Now I just have to go home and wait for the knock on my door.

CHAPTER EIGHTEEN

Emmy

My fingertips brush the doorknob, but I pull back my hand. Is this really a good idea? *You've already done it once before*, I tell myself. *Just one more time.* I close my eyes and take a deep breath, and then, against my better judgment, I open the door to Dale's office.

A fan hums in the corner, backlit by the computer monitor showcasing a picture of Dale on a fishing trip. What I need stands behind all of that, beneath a stack of papers a mile high. I've watched my boss punch in the code to that safe one thousand times, and I know what's just behind that locked door—a way out.

While I'm not proud of what I'm about to do, I don't see another solution. If I didn't care about Benji, he'd be the perfect out, but I've developed some feelings I'm not ready to deal with yet. The thought of Jessie hurting him because of me . . . it's too much to bear. The only escape that makes sense is if I just grab some cash, take my kitten, and get the hell out of this town. Homelessness would be better at this point.

"Maybe just take a little each week," I whisper. "Not so much that Dale will notice, but enough to tuck away."

I'm already doing the math in my head as I kneel in front of the safe. I could stick it out for another month if I'm careful—both with Jessie and with this thievery. I feel bad because Dale was nice enough to give me this job despite my history, and now I'm proving that recidivism is at an all-time high. It's not my fucking fault I keep getting into the most desperate situations known to man. If someone has a problem with it, they should take it up with whoever put my life on hard mode.

The safe door releases with a puff of air. I'm in.

I make a mental note of where everything is in the safe so that I can put it back correctly when I'm finished. He keeps the big bills in a large black-velvet sack, so I snag a couple of those before stuffing some smaller bills into my pockets. There isn't time to count. All the other staff are gone for the night, but he's out back taking his smoke break, which can last anywhere from ten minutes to the rest of the night.

I've just closed the safe when I hear footsteps outside in the hall. In a panic, I dart for the door, but the jingle of keys just outside tells me I'm too late. My eyes scan the room for any excuse that explains why I'm in here, but I come up with nothing.

Maybe he'll just keep walking . . .

The door opens like a nightmare, letting in a sliver of light that shines on me in spotlight fashion. Dale and I both shout and jump back, though I'm the only one still shaking as he enters the office and cuts on the light.

"Emmy, I thought you went home already. What are you doing in here?"

My brain prepares a lie, but my heart is too tired. I'm going through entirely too much shit, and I can't take another step. So I pull the money from my pockets and drop it onto the desk. I tell him everything. Well, maybe not everything. I don't tell him that my boyfriend is beating me, but I let him know I'm in a bad situation.

As he listens, his face softens. He sits at his desk, nodding and almost seeming to sympathize. Now I don't know why I didn't just come to him with all of this in the first place. He's being incredibly reasonable.

He shakes his head and sits forward. "Emmy, I don't have to tell you how bad it would look if I went to your probation officer about this."

"I know." Tears fill my eyes again. "It's selfish of me to ask, but could this stay between us? I'll find another job."

"You won't find another job in this town with your record." He shakes his head again, slower this time. "No, I'll keep you employed here. And I want you to have the money."

My eyes widen. He can't be serious. "Dale, I can't accept that."

"You'll accept it." A cunning look darkens his eyes. "But how badly do you want me to keep quiet?"

I understand what he's getting at almost immediately, but my brain has checked out. No part of my consciousness wants to accept that we have jumped from the frying pan to the fire. Rock bottom is heading for me faster than I can brace for impact.

"Why don't you come over here and sit on my lap while we talk about it?" He pats his jean-clad thigh and smiles at me.

On wooden legs, I do as he asks. I sit on his lap as he brushes my hair from my shoulder. I let his hands wander. I cry through all of it. As his fingertips run over my body, the tears hurry to wash away the feel of his touch. I stare at the picture on his computer and imagine I'm there. I'm in that water, swimming away from everyone who hurts me. Escape would be a miracle. Death would be a blessing.

My eyes close against the pain of intrusion. I've known too much of this lately. Now I'm starting to wonder if I'll ever know anything else.

Benji . . .

Darkness gives way to light in my mind, and I slip away to another place. It's quiet there, no need for words. His arms are around me. He won't let them hurt me anymore. He won't—

Dale finishes on the floor. He's kind enough to tell me he'll worry about the cleanup. With a grunt, he stuffs the cash into my hand and tells me he'll see me at work tomorrow.

"And don't worry," he adds with a wink. "This stays between us . . . so long as you keep up with your end of the bargain."

I nod and leave his office. Great. So this wasn't a one-off. Now I'll be abused at home *and* at work. Fucking fabulous.

With a pocketful of money I no longer want, I hurry toward the bus stop. My hair and makeup are a mess, but if I'm going to Benji's like he told me to, it won't matter. He won't care that I look like I feel inside. Jessie, on the other hand, will accuse me of doing exactly what I just did, only in his mind, it was consensual on my side. Even if I told him Dale essentially raped me via coercion, he'd just blame me.

I cover my face with my hands. "What a mess," I whisper into my palms. "What a fucking mess."

Benji may not care what I look like, but he might care that another man has been inside me. His brother doesn't seem to matter, but Dale? If he's anything like his brother, Benji will find some way to spin it so that it was all my fault. He's not like his brother, though. He's everything Jessie pretends to be. He's all the goodness and none of the malice. How did I ever think Jessie was the better catch?

The bus pulls up, and I'm faced with a decision. Do I go to Benji with this, or do I keep yet another secret until it tears me apart?

My feet clack up the steps. I take a seat near the back and pray no one can see the pain on my face. Lights drift by outside the window, and my decision approaches. It shouldn't be this difficult, but I haven't been doing well in the decision department lately. That has a way of shaking your confidence.

But as the bus rolls on, I know exactly where I need to go.

CHAPTER NINETEEN

BENJI

She should have been here by now. Her shift ended an hour ago, and even if Dale needed her to stick around until he locked up, I should have her in my arms. Since I don't, I guess it's safe to assume she's not coming. Unlike my brother, I won't chase her down and force her to heel like a dog. If she comes to me, I want it willingly. Being chosen has always been more desirable than forcing someone to choose me.

That's what Jessie does. He breaks the spirit. He isn't chosen; he's tolerated.

My stomach grumbles, and I'm not in the mood to cook anything, so I order a pizza from one of two places open this late. I get one half with double pepperoni and extra sauce, just like she likes it. Just in case.

Yet again, I'm being an embarrassment to myself, longing for the girl I can't have. Doing sweet shit like ordering half the pizza her way when she won't even be here to eat it. I feel like a moron for hoping against hope that she'll show. Then I feel like an *asshole* for hoping against hope that she'll show.

She's my brother's girlfriend, and regardless of what he's done to her, we're both betraying him by continuing anything physical. Her safety is my number-one concern, but right on its tail is number-two: throwing her onto the bed and eating her pussy until she can't walk. It's wrong, and we should stop.

But I won't stop, so it's probably a good thing that she went home to him.

It's unfair and a little selfish of me to take advantage of her when she's vulnerable, but the timing isn't my fucking problem. This girl is my one chance at happiness, even if it's short-lived. If my brother would just set her free, I could be happy forever. She doesn't even have to be with me. She just has to be free.

I hear a knock on the door and grab a ten to tip the driver. It feels good to have money to tip with. Back when I relied solely on Jessie for my finances, this would have been impossible. He still hasn't handed off my disability checks, but I'm considering handling it on my own, anyway. I used to think letting him help me out was good for him, that it made him feel more like part of my life. Now I realize I've been as unwitting as the women he's abused. He's only seen it as a means of control. That's fine. I know where to go and who to talk to about getting things moved to a private account.

Shit, maybe I could just start dumping that check and letting it sit. When it's built up enough, I'll grab Emmy and her kitten and take off for somewhere he won't find either of us. Hell, I'll tie her to the fucking passenger seat if I have to, and when we get where we're going, I'll ask what she wants.

If that isn't me, I'll leave, and I'll still have a smile on my face.

So long as it isn't him. So long as she's okay.

Even as I open the door, I hope Emmy will be waiting on the other side. Instead, I'm greeted by an older woman with coke-bottle glasses. She holds the pizza toward me.

"That'll be seventeen even," she says.

I hand her the twenty and a ten.

"Oh, I don't have any change," she says, and I motion for her to take what I gave her and leave. She gets the message and thanks me before shuffling back to her car.

I shut the door behind me and take my sad pizza to the couch. The more I think about what Emmy might be enduring right now, the more my appetite recedes. Are they making up at this very moment? Or is he beating her again?

Another knock on the door drags me out of my thoughts. It's probably just that lady giving me change.

But when I open the door, Emmy is standing there. "Hey," she says, and her voice is so small.

"Is something wrong?" I ask. "I didn't think you'd come."

But her concern overpowers mine when she notices the gash on my cheek from my little altercation with my brother. Realization dawns in her eyes. "Why would you do this for me?"

The question hurts. Does she genuinely think she's not worth every bit of this agony? Why can't she see that I'd lie on a bed of razor wire if it meant she could walk over me to get away from my brother? I'd do more if I could, but short of killing him, this was the best I could manage.

She leans closer as she examines my face. I raise my hands to sign something, but she interrupts me as her lips press to mine. Her face against mine fucking hurts, and when her body presses against me next, it makes my entire ribcage ache. But I couldn't care less. I've hurt enough for a lifetime. What's a little more?

"Finish what you didn't earlier," she whispers against my mouth.

"Not until you tell me why you've been crying," I sign. As soon as I've finished, my hands go to her cheeks, where I brush back the mascara smudges. "Darling . . . what happened to you?"

Fresh tears fill her eyes, and she leaps into my arms, knocking me backward into the apartment. Her mouth melds with mine, and the passion behind her kiss makes me ache to hold her closer. I kick the door shut behind me and place her feet on the floor. She tries to kiss me again, but I hold up my hands and lead her to the couch.

"Did you go to his house first? Did he hurt you again?" I ask, but she shakes her head. "Why don't you leave him? You don't have to be with me, but you *shouldn't* be with him."

"It's not that easy."

Then it dawns on me. "What is he holding over you? Is it money?"

"Don't ask me that," she whispers.

I feel her anxiety. It's slow, creeping like a poison. My chest tightens as if a hand is grasping my heart. Her emotions bleed into me, the tension rushing faster and harder, and I feel each pulse of her panic as if it were my own. I just can't find the source of the problem. Without that, how can I stem the forceful flow of hurt pouring out of her now?

"I can't help you if I don't know what's wrong."

"I don't need help, Benji."

My fingers trace her throat, and I feel her swallow. "Tell me what he has over you, darling. Let me in."

She blinks away a tear, and I trace its path down the curve of her jaw. "I did something to help my brother keep his scholarship, and somehow, your brother found out."

"Did you rob a bank or something?"

A small laugh leaves her lips before she becomes stone again. "Worse. I robbed my place of employment. I'm on a prison deferral program, and if I lose the job I have right now, I have to go back into custody. I don't regret what I did. My brother overcame so much, and I didn't want a little poverty to come between him and his next big thing." Her shoulders rise in a tiny shrug. "So . . ."

"If you leave him, he'll ruin you?"

"That's what he said."

Fuck. That's a big enough something to keep Emmy at his side through every hit, choke, or punch. That anxiety crushes my heart in my chest again, and it's not hers this time. It's mine. I knew that fucking her was wrong on a biblical level, but my selfish desire to have her trumped any morals I once held. Now I realize I can't have her. Not even if I fall on my sword and bleed at her feet. She'd just go home to my brother with my blood on her shoes.

"See?" she whispers. "I'm not a good person. I deserve everything that's happening to me."

Now I know why she was so eager to have her mouth on mine. She needs to feel something. It's the same reason I cut.

Sometimes, words aren't the right answer after all.

I lay her down on my couch and climb over her. My hand brushes back the red strands of hair covering her soft cheek. Her eyelashes flutter, and she licks her lips as her gaze meets mine.

"We're so broken," I sign.

"Broken," she whispers.

"For tonight, let this fix us."

I ease off our clothes, careful of the many bruises between us. She gasps and places her fingertips over my ribs when she sees the gnarly marks there, and I place my fingertips on her cheek.

We've both been hurt by the same hand, we say to each other. No signs are needed. No words. Only presence, and we're both here right now.

I spread her thighs around me and gaze down at her. The lighting in this room is terrible, yet she still looks so perfectly *fuckable* beneath me. Leaning over, I place my hand behind her head and draw her lips to mine, letting my pierced tongue roll over hers. Her hands move over my chest. My abs. They find what they seek, and she smiles against my lips as she grips my girth. Then her thumb drags over the piercings, and she lets out the softest whimper.

I lean back and gather spit beneath my tongue, and the warm string clings to my lower lip before dropping to the heat between her legs. I press my tip to her entrance and push my hips forward, and she moans as I slip inside her.

"Good fucking girl," I sign. I rock my hips forward again, and I earn another glorious moan. "Just like that, darling."

My hands are about to be much too busy for words, so I hope she'll forgive my silence. One is now buried in her hair, and the other is drawing back her pussy lips so that I can see my piercings catch against her. And that's what happens. I feed her, inch by inch, until she has to stretch around the metal balls to swallow what I give her. That whimper of pleasurable pain nearly makes me lose myself inside her.

I lean forward and kiss her. *Fuck,* I mouth against her lips. She whimpers, and I open my mouth to breathe in her next moan as I push deep inside her. This girl gives me everything I anticipate and more. She moans into my mouth and arches her back, grinding herself against my pelvis.

I've never felt something like being inside her. It's as if she's a balm to my aching bones. She heals some wounded part of me and mends my shattered soul. Being inside her is more than I can bear, yet it's the very thing that gives me the will to take my next breath. There will be no other reason after this. What we've experienced before this was only a taste of the pleasures that awaited us. Even now, we're only at the cusp of whatever this could be.

There's something special about feeling this good after a whole lot of pain. It's a contradiction; it shouldn't exist. But it does. And I can't keep my eyes off her a moment longer as I curl my hips into hers. She moans, and I drop my hand between her legs. She reaches down and pulls my hand away.

"Just fuck me. *Use* me."

"Darling—"

"Make me feel wanted."

Thank god I only need one hand to sign what I want to say. "I need you."

Her eyes close, and a moan rolls from her lips. I reward her by fucking her harder. Faster. Until every thrust hurts me as much as it pleases me. I give her exactly what she begged for, and I *use* her.

My balls tighten, and I'm going to come. I've never wanted anything more than to fill her.

But the rush of guilt kicks me in my bruised fucking rib, and I think of my brother at the very moment I'm prepared to make her mine.

I cage her within my arms and drop my face to her neck. "What's wrong, Benji?"

Her voice is a whispered worry. *Did I do something wrong? Did I fuck this up?* These are the questions she's probably asking herself. I can't let her think it's anything she's done. She needs to understand that if she really wants this from me, it means she's choosing me. Asking to be chosen isn't easy, but I'll be damned if I chase a woman who doesn't choose me.

If she says no, that it's him, I'll stop right now. I'll end the obsession. I'll never stop caring for her, and I'll continue to protect her. But I will let her go.

If she says yes, if she chooses me, then I will fuck and fill her and *never* let her go. I will possess her in ways my brother is incapable of. She will be cherished, adored, and worshipped.

Nightly.

I sit up and look down at her. I brush the sweat from her brow. Then I sigh. "This is wrong. I shouldn't want you this way when—"

"Everything about this fucking life is wrong. Your bruises. Mine. This." She winds her legs around my waist and raises her hips, rocking me inside her. "Make it worse, Benji. I *need* you to want me the way I want you."

"You want me?"

"From the moment I met your brother."

Shit, that's enough for me.

I drop forward and kiss her. My hips grind into her, and pleasure ignites between us again. There is no gentle start, no easing into it. Her body begs me to take, so I do. My hips hammer forward, occasionally ramming in and grinding upward *real* slow. Just so I can watch her eyes roll back. My arms burn as they hold up my weight. I won't stop, though.

The bones can snap and the muscles can liquefy, and I will still find a way to maintain this position. I've never felt anything so incredible, so fucking perfect. Then her words echo in my ears. That sweet voice tells me once again that she *needs* me to want her.

And with her admission soothing my guilt, I make her mine.

I fill my brother's girlfriend.

And I wish I felt worse about it.

CHAPTER TWENTY

EMMY

How do two entirely broken beings fit together like this? That's the question I keep asking myself as I lie in Benji's bed, held within his arms. His jagged pieces fit into every part of me that Jessie has torn open. When he kisses me, I seem to forget about everything.

That's why I didn't mention anything about Dale.

I wanted to. I had planned to come here and tell Benji everything—about my past *and* present problems—but when I saw that massive bruise on his side, I no longer felt that telling Benji would be safe for him. Hell, now I'm scared to tell him if *Jessie* acts up. I don't want someone I care about to take a hit for me.

Besides, Dale won't be a future problem. I hope. Maybe no one ever needs to know about what happened in that office.

"My brother is so fucking stupid," he signs.

"Forget him right now," I whisper. "Let's just have this moment of peace before it all goes to hell again. We should probably get some sleep. We're both on in the morning tomorrow."

Benji sits up with a smile. "Oh no, darling. We aren't sleeping tonight. I'm going to show you what my brother is incapable of. Besides, I wouldn't get to see you for six to eight hours because I don't have dreams."

"You still need sleep."

"And miss out on this time with you?" He shakes his head and signs, "N-O! Not a fucking chance."

I smile and reach beneath the blanket to touch him, but my hand grazes the cut on his thigh. He winces, and I do as well when I feel the warm wetness on my fingertips. I guess our earlier activities opened the wound. "You're bleeding again."

He looks almost embarrassed, but I don't want him to feel shame. There's nothing shameful about needing an outlet for your pain, even if it's an unhealthy one. Shit, just look at me.

"I know how I can help you sleep." I nibble my lip and trace my finger over his lap. He's separated from my touch by a thin comforter.

He smirks and signs, "I don't know if I could stay in control right now."

"Then don't."

His smirk falls. "I don't want to hurt you, not even if that pain precedes an ungodly amount of pleasure."

"I'm sick of feeling numb," I sign back. "Make me feel something. Anything."

I raise the blanket and dip beneath it before he can argue. In the warm, dark confines, I find the cut and bring my lips to his thigh. This isn't anything I've ever thought about doing, but now that I'm here, it's the most intimate thing I've ever experienced. My tongue meets with a metallic warmth, and I swirl my way through salt and skin. His cock jumps beside my face, and Benji sucks in a breath.

His hand finds my hair. With a firm grip, he pulls my head from beneath the blanket. "I'm sorry," he signs when he releases my head.

"You don't have to apologize for that," I say, motioning to the cut.

"No, not for that. I'm sorry for what I'm about to do to your beautiful mouth."

His hand winds through my hair again, and he guides my head toward his cock. What he does next isn't gentle or romantic, but it's definitely passionate. His desire, his *need*, pulses in my throat with each thrust of his hips. He rams my head onto his cock, punishing me as I requested.

It's different when it's what I want. Jessie and Dale used me until nothing was left, but being used by Benji is more like being cherished. Very roughly.

Tears stream down my cheeks as I gag and choke on his unrelenting cock. These are the only tears he'll allow me to shed—tears of pleasure. When he snatches my head away from his lap and looks down at me, the glassy, pleasure-driven sheen in his eyes makes my thighs clench. He releases my head so that he can sign to me.

"You're so fucking sexy, darling. My brother doesn't tell you that, does he?"

I shake my head.

"I bet he doesn't worship your body the way it deserves, huh?"

Again, I shake my head.

"Then let me do what he can't. My brother will never know your worth. He doesn't deserve your body."

And with that, he's on me. His mouth captures mine, and I feel each of his facial piercings in Technicolor. His hands go from my face to my neck. They wrap around my throat, but I don't shy away from his touch. I lean into the warmth across my throat. This isn't Jessie's hand. This is safe.

His fingers curl around the flesh and cut off the blood to my head. A hot feeling rushes over me, and I gasp as the warmth almost comforts me. He kisses me through it all. His hands aren't a threat. They're bringers of pleasure. They're his voice.

They're my salvation.

He breaks the kiss and slides down my body. "Go place your hands on the door. I want you standing. Let me worship you, darling."

I move to the door, fully expecting him to come up and start railing me. I'm shocked when I hear him drop to his knees behind me. As I peer between my legs, I can just see his cock standing stiff between his thighs. His hands grip my legs as he pulls me closer, and my eyes roll the moment his tongue ring dances over my clit. I've never felt anything like it. He leaves a trail of electrical shocks between my legs as he lashes me with his tongue.

My waist bends a bit more, giving me a better view of his cock as he pleasures me. He isn't stroking himself, but his shaft throbs as if he's getting close. That's impossible, but the thought is enough to send me barreling toward an orgasm.

But then his cock spasms, and his pleasure spurts onto the floor. It's too much. Knowing how I affect him is too much. My nails drive into the door as the orgasm overtakes my body.

"Fuck, Benji," I pant. "I'm coming."

He keeps eating me until I nearly collapse, but the orgasm won't stop. I keep replaying that moment when he came from going down on me. His hands were on me, and there was no friction anywhere near him. I've never felt more desired.

The high finally begins to ebb, and he steadies me before cleaning me up with nothing more than his tongue. He bites his lip as he looks down at the mess on the floor.

"Did that really just happen?" I ask, still in shock.

"It happens every time I eat your pussy, darling. I don't even need to touch myself. I just need *you*."

As we head back to the bed, I'm starting to understand why he doesn't want to sleep. Suddenly, I don't want to sleep either. Because when I wake up, this will end. I'll have to go back to the monster waiting for me at home. Then I remember the monster waiting for me at work, and it's more than I can bear.

But then I look at Benji. Maybe, with his help, I can bear it just a little longer.

CHAPTER TWENTY-ONE

BENJI

The secret meetings with Emmy consume my every waking thought. For the past two weeks, we've been sneaking around behind Jessie's back, meeting any chance we could. Sometimes she shows up crying. She denies that it's because of Jessie, but what else could it be? I haven't seen any more marks on her body, but not all abuse is visible.

I want him to treat her better, but that's a double-edged sword. If he treats her better, she might decide he's the better option. He's the one with the nice house, multiple cars, and a stacked bank account. He's the standout, Mr. Personality, the one who lights up a room. I'm . . . none of those things.

I can give her something he can't, though. I can love her more than I love myself, and Jessie will never be capable of something so selfless.

What I feel for her has to be love. No other word comes close.

She's the first person I want to come to with good news. She's the last voice I want to hear before I sleep at night. All of the goodness and none of the bad—that's Emmy Lewis.

And right on cue, she strolls from the back of the restaurant with a tray held above her head. Her red ponytail swishes behind her, matching the sway of her hips. I lower the bus tub and just enjoy the view for a moment. Feeling my stare, she turns and gives me a sly smile. I see a little supply-closet session in our near future.

She greets the table—a happy family of three—and places their plates in front of them. The little kid says something, and Emmy smiles. Her infectious joy spreads, and the parents smile too. She has that effect on people. Goodness is drawn to her.

But badness is drawn to her too. Men like my brother see all that sweetness, and they want to break it down. They want to overpower and ridicule and change her.

Then there's me, somewhere in between. I'm drawn to her goodness, but I'm not perfect. I have secrets, and I've done things I'm ashamed of. Or I guess I should say, I'm ashamed of the things I didn't do. That I couldn't do.

Emmy's smile falls, and she schools her face as Dale steps near the table. He's probably asking the family how they're enjoying the meal they haven't even had a chance to bite into yet. I shake my head. That guy is such an idiot.

We finish out the shift with a few more flirty glances and a secret message or two across the dining room. Families and drunk barflies head home, and servers leave one by one until only Emmy, Dale, and I remain. I'm not slated to close—he's been scheduling Emmy more and more often for that awful job—but I stick around to ask Emmy if I can drive her home tonight. I can't always— that would just make Jessie suspicious—but every now and then, she agrees.

That usually means a quick pit stop by my place, which we could both use tonight. It's been a long shift.

But as I stand by the supply closet, left with nothing more than my thoughts, I start really considering what a mess I'm in. Getting the disability payment back into my hands? That was a bust. There was too much red tape to cut through, and it would have taken too long. Emmy doesn't have that kind of time. We're lucky things have seemed so calm lately. The serene feelings were only skin deep, though.

Because while I've never been happier than in these moments I've shared with Emmy, I've never been more miserable than in these moments I've languished without her.

I thought I could accept only having her sometimes, but sometimes isn't enough. What's my alternative, though? Losing her completely?

There are nights I damn near need to handcuff myself to the bed frame to stop my legs from carrying me to her. Not just for my own selfish uses, either. Sometimes I just long to know she's okay. It starts as an idea and grows into a beast that nags me until I pick up my phone and beg myself to stop. Because if I send a text, that might end both our lives.

My fingers start itching for a blade to run down my leg. I need to feel something other than whatever this is. I hate it.

The walls are closing in, and I should get my mind elsewhere before I do something I'll regret. Maybe I can find Emmy and help her with whatever side work has her bogged down.

I leave the hall and check the back booth where she usually preps silverware, but she isn't there. She isn't in the back breaking down boxes or slicing lemons for the next day, either. I pull out my phone to text her as I come back up the hall, and that's when I slam into a body. I look up and see that it's Emmy.

Her ponytail hangs askew, the same way it usually does on the nights when she shows up crying. Makeup runs down her beautiful cheeks, but she's already swiped away the tears that formed the dark tracks. She shakes her head and turns to walk away from me. My stomach tightens at the familiar shame in her eyes. And as Dale comes out of his office, still buttoning his pants, the dots connect and form a picture I don't want to look at too closely.

That look on Emmy's face is so familiar because I had that same look on my face whenever I left Mr. Ormsby's classroom.

Dale gives me a wave and a pinched smile as he shuffles past. I go in the opposite direction, hurrying after Emmy. I grab her shoulder to stop her once I catch her.

"What did he do to you?"

She closes her eyes and shakes her head again.

I grip her chin until she opens her eyes. "Tell me what he did to you. I know it wasn't your choice."

Her chin quivers as she raises her hands and signs, "It's my fault. I fucked up. I did this to myself."

Rage fills me. The thought of him touching her brings me back to a terribly dark place, but him making her think this is somehow her fault pushes me past the edge of sanity. I pull her into me. His disgusting lips have probably been on hers. His cock was inside what's mine.

She pulls back. "If you never want to touch me again, I'll understand," she signs through silent sobs. "I'm dirty. I'm used."

I grip her shoulders and shake her, and when I raise my

hands to speak, I pour everything I feel into my movements, my face. I may not have a voice, but she will hear me loud and clear. "You are the purest thing I have ever known. If you feel dirty, I will bathe you in my adoration until you feel clean. If you feel used, let it be me who uses you. *Nothing* can lower your value in my eyes."

"Please," she whines. "Please show me that I'm not worthless now."

"I'm going to make you mine once more, and then I'll make sure he *never* makes you cry again."

"You can't!" Her hands fly in front of her as her eyes widen. "You don't understand."

She glances around, then grabs my hand and leads me into the supply closet. Then she explains that she snuck into Dale's office, that he caught her, and what he now holds over her head. She's right to feel it's an impossible situation. For most people, it would be, but I have the solution. It's drastic, but sometimes a man has to take that step. Even if that step is off of a cliff, if it means saving her, he walks forward with his head held high.

Yeah, what I'm thinking of will probably end about the same way. There will be no open casket for Benji. So long as it's the kick in the pants Emmy needs to get her away from Jessie, this is a sacrifice I'm happy to make. If this is my last night on the planet, though, I know how I want it to end.

I wipe the makeup from under her eyes and kiss her. Another man's touch won't stop me from branding my touch deeper. Not my brother's. Not Dale's. I'm angry. I'm fucking pissed about how horribly these men have failed her. But that doesn't make me want her any less.

A tear slips down her cheek, and I lean into her and press my tongue to the salty bead. I want her sadness inside me. I want to feel it too. My lips melt against hers again, and I kiss away any remnant of another man.

I work down my black jeans, then ease off her pants. Our shattered pieces come together as I lift her leg and push my cock inside her. She gasps against my lips as I back her into the wall and knock over a broom. I catch it before it clatters, then cage her within my arms so that I can give her all of me. I want to please her and make her forget the harms she's endured.

She moans into my mouth, and while I can't speak, I let that be my voice for the moment. My pleasure is tethered to hers, and that rope pulls taut with every thrust. When she comes around me, I feel every earth-shattering, mind-bending spasm as she squeezes my cock in a vise. My orgasm follows hers, almost arriving on the same breath, and fuck, that ruins me. Absolutely breaks me. Because we are so in tune with each other. Because this is the sort of connection that comes along once in your life.

And what I plan to do once Emmy leaves for the night will be the end of mine.

With a sigh, she gives me a sad smile and kisses me. Now comes the hard part. If I tell her what I plan to do tonight, she'll never let me go through with it. So I do the worst thing possible. I lie to her. I tell her I'm too angry to drive her home tonight, but that I promise to be good.

It's a promise I can't keep. Especially not as I stuff something hard and heavy down the back of my pants.

After I walk her to the bus stop and wait for her bus to arrive, I slink back to the parking lot. Dale's dinosaur of a sedan is still parked out back, right in the darkest area, and how very fucking convenient for me that there aren't any cameras back here. I squat down, pull the lace from my shoe, and make quick work of the ancient door latch through the cracked window. Then I slip into the back seat. The all-black attire makes hiding pretty simple. Once I duck down a bit, he won't even know I'm here unless he peers into the floorboard.

I don't have to wait long before Dale comes strolling out the back door, a cigarette between his fingers. Worried he might spot me, I duck down a bit more. Smoke dances around me as he climbs inside and puts the car in drive, and off we go.

I'm not dumb enough to kill him at work. There are far too many cameras around the front of the building, and I'm only thankful Dale doesn't give enough of a shit about his staff to put any in the back. I'm also not dumb enough to kill him at his house, where I could leave a metric fuck ton of evidence behind, so I wait and I watch the window for the perfect moment. As we approach some farmland, I spring from the back and wave in the rearview mirror.

"Benji!" Dale screams when he spots me. He swerves before regaining control of the car. "What the hell are you doing here?"

There's no good way to do this as someone without a voice. I'm incapable of delivering a heart-wrenching speech or even something as simple as an explanation. But that's okay. I don't need a voice to get this message across.

I raise the hammer from the shadows and bring it down. Dale ducks out of the way, and the blocky metal tool slams onto his shoulder. Something snaps under the force, and the car swerves into a field as he dodges the next blow. He begins to slow the vehicle, clearly planning to tuck and roll, but I don't have time for a foot chase.

The hammer comes down again, and a satisfying *crunch* greets me as his skull caves. His fingers flex before dropping uselessly into his lap, but it's not enough. I bring the hammer down again and again, even as the car picks up speed. A chunk of bloodstained bone flies free and lands in my lap, and only then do I finally stop swinging.

We aren't going that fast, but it's enough to give me a nasty jolt when I pull the parking brake. I had every intention of going down with the car, but if I can walk away from this, that sounds even better.

Dale flops to the side. His chest heaves, weaker and weaker. Blood drains from the hole in his skull, like pouring thick red milk from a jug. I would have loved to have told him what he was doing was disgusting. Wrong. Just like what my abuser did to me.

But no one will steal Emmy's voice. I made sure of that.

With the thoughts of my abuser fresh in my mind, I start swinging on this dead man's head again. I pretend it's Mr. Ormsby.

When he asked me to stay after class like I'd done something wrong.

When he gave me dessert cakes as a "reward" like I'd done something right.

When he . . .

When he did irreparable harm to me and my psyche.

I hit Dale until he isn't recognizable anymore. Not as a human being. And somehow, it still isn't enough, so I flip the hammer around and stab the claw into his crotch.

I wish Emmy could be here for this . . .

But as my chest heaves, as I look down at what I've done and what I've become, I don't think I want her here at all. I've never killed anyone before—only nearly killed myself— but I always knew I had it in me. If she saw me right now, she'd probably think I look just like Jessie.

If she saw me right now, she'd probably never speak to me again.

CHAPTER TWENTY-TWO

Emmy

Being around Jessie has become unbearable. I have to play nice and pretend I'm still in love when I have one foot out the door. I do whatever it takes to avoid the next fight that could land me in the hospital. Sometimes I wonder if just letting Jessie put me in prison would be better than the name calling. The abuse. The dread.

But it's not all dread.

Because of one person and one person only—his brother.

If I had chosen him instead of Jessie, maybe everything would be different.

"Hey, baby?" Jessie calls from the bedroom.

"Yes?"

I sink into the couch and stroke Lily's fur as I wish I wasn't a living being. If I could be a lamp right now, that would be great. My throat tenses as I hold back impending tears. No matter how much I hate him, he holds my world in an iron fist. He can put me away. Even if I tried to put him there first, who would the police believe? Him or the felon? A police officer would need to witness my murder for me to have any chance of getting him put away for a fucking year.

His footsteps drift closer. "You haven't already started dinner? I'm starving."

"I'll do it right now." I hurry to the kitchen, not even daring to see if he's being amicable or if he's already pissed. It's impossible to tell from the sound of his voice alone.

I'm not really hungry as I pull things from cupboards and drawers. I start a pot of water for spaghetti, figuring I can throw together some meatballs with the leftover ground beef in the fridge. After a quick sniff test to make sure the meat hasn't gone bad, I start forming balls with some panko and milk. My mother taught me the milk trick.

Lily jumps from a chair to a table, then onto the counter. She pokes her wiggling nose against my meat-coated hands. She's only recently started counter surfing, but it's a habit I need to break.

"No, silly girl." I giggle and nudge her away with my elbow. I don't want to get raw meat all over her fur, so I cover the bowl and go to the sink to wash my hands.

While my back is turned, I hear the bowl clatter to the tiles, accompanied by the most horrific sound I've ever heard an animal make. I spin around, expecting to find Lily surrounded by glass and blood on the floor, but it's so much worse. The glass bowl has shattered, but Lily isn't on the floor. She's being held up by her tail as Jessie suspends her midair in his brutal fist.

Lily continues to yowl in pain as he grits his teeth and squeezes. He stares at her the same way he's stared at me. Contempt blazes like fire in his eyes.

"Jessie, let her go!" I scream. I rush forward to support

her weight, but he backhands me and sends me into the counter.

"Why would you let that filthy piece of shit near our food?" He shakes her a final time before flinging her sideways. She lands on her feet and skitters down the hall, toward the bedroom.

Every cell of my being screams for me to check on her, but I don't move a muscle. I grip the counter and remain still. Even when he brushes my hair from my shoulder, I don't move.

"She's a goddamn cat, Emmy. You aren't mad about that, are you?" He kisses my shoulder, and I close my eyes.

"No, not mad," I say, and I'm surprised when my voice doesn't quiver like a newborn fawn. That's how I feel inside. Weak. Small. "But she's a kitten, Jessie."

He laughs, sending a puff of warm air over my skin. "If she's so important to you, then don't let her filthy ass sit on my fucking countertops." He gives my ass a firm pat. "Finish making dinner."

One of the worst things I've ever had to do is go back to some mundane activity like cooking dinner while the equivalent of my child cowers in pain beneath the bed. But I do it. I go through the motions and finish cooking and serving him dinner. I can't even pick at my food because my appetite evaporated the moment I heard his voice.

"You need to take that cat to a shelter tonight. I'll let you use my car." He raises his glass and takes a sip. "Just like that job, she's been nothing but a point of contention for us."

I see an out, so I seize it. "You're probably right. It would be for the best."

A plan starts forming in my mind. I'm off work for three days, so Dale wouldn't be able to report me to the probation office until then. I'll pack up the kitten's things and then drive Jessie's car until the gas runs out. Then I'll walk until my legs give out. It's the best solution for everyone. No more Jessie. No more Dale. Lily would be safe, and so would I.

And so would Benji.

I go to stand, but Jessie places his hand over mine. "Not until you clean that plate." He points to my uneaten meal as I sit down once more. Then he brushes my hair to the side and leans closer. "I'm glad you're being such a good girl now, Emmy. Isn't this nice?"

With a small smile at him, I nod and pick up my fork. It's a form of torture to make someone eat under duress. Each mechanical motion is monumental and exhausting, and my stomach twists the moment the first bite hits my tongue. I just keep reliving that terrible sound Lily made when he snatched her off the counter and shook her by her tail. I'm absolutely sickened by it.

I force down every bite of food and clean our plates before grabbing the small carrier and coaxing Lily inside it. Her tail is kinked at the end, so I can only assume it's broken. I pull her against my chest and utter silent apologies into her soft fur. We're stopping at the first vet office I find once we're out of this state. I don't care if it takes every penny I've scrounged; I won't let anything hurt Lily again.

Once I've bundled all of her food and things into a bag, I tuck the envelope containing my meager savings inside a bag of cat food and head for Jessie's car. My hands shake, and tears stream down my face as I back up and start down the long driveway. Is this really happening? Am I really doing this?

The car picks up speed as I travel down the road. The turn for the animal shelter passes by on my right, but I don't slow down. Did he really think I'd leave her in their drop pen overnight? I look at the carrier. There is no way.

My phone rings, and I look down at it. It's Jessie. In my blind panic, muscle memory kicks in, and I answer the call.

"You're going the wrong way," he says into the phone, and my blood runs cold. "The tracker on the car says you passed the animal shelter."

Shit.

I should have seen this coming, but in my excitement to escape this hell I'm in, I didn't even consider it. Of course Jessie has a tracker on his fucking car.

"Yeah, I'm just not comfortable leaving her at the shelter, so I'm taking her to your brother. Is that okay?" I wince. Do I care if he thinks it's okay? No. But I also have to keep the control in his hands. "If it's not okay with you, I'll just take her and drop her off. It's whatever you want."

He thinks this over, then says, "No, that's fine. Benji needs something to keep him company, I guess. Why not another expense he can't afford?"

"Oh, you're right," I say, though I roll my eyes. God help me if he has a camera in here. "Maybe that isn't a good idea."

"I don't give a shit where the cat goes so long as you don't bring it back here. Just get your fine ass back to my bed as quickly as possible. I need to reward you for being so good tonight." He hangs up the phone.

Whatever the reward is, I don't want it.

The intersection approaches, and now I don't know which way to turn, both literally and figuratively. If I go right, I head toward Benji. I sink him even further inside this shitstorm I've created. If I go left, I drive until Jessie calls the cops and reports the car as stolen. Prison is looking like a vacation at this point.

So I put on the blinker, and I make a choice.

CHAPTER TWENTY-THREE

Benji

This apartment is entirely too quiet without Emmy. I miss her laughter. Her voice. There isn't even a chance to communicate. If I text her first, that could be the catalyst for her next set of injuries.

Maybe I should just drive by and check on her. Maybe I can catch a glimpse of her through the window again. I grab the keys and pick up my jacket before I open the front door. I don't expect to see Emmy coming up the walkway with a pet carrier under her arm. Why is she here?

I start signing, but she rushes past me in a flurry of wild red hair.

"He hurt her!" she yells, her voice strained. "Now he's tracking me. This is a mess."

She stops in the living room and puts the carrier on the floor. I close the front door, and she frees her tiny captive. The fluffy gray kitten tiptoes from inside with wide, wild eyes. Emmy looks absolutely gutted as she strokes the kitten's back. The pain is something I so intimately recognize. It's the way I feel when I look at her when she's hurt.

"What happened?" I sign.

"She jumped on the counter, and Jessie ripped her off by the tail. The sound she made . . . Benji, I'll never forget that horrible sound!"

I don't particularly love cats. In fact, I'm pretty fucking allergic. But I walk over to her and put my hand on the soft fur. I rub my hand down her back, and her hair prickles beneath my fingers. That's when I notice her tail. This is a new low, even for my brother.

"She can stay with me."

"I planned to ask, but I remember you said that you're allergic to them. Do you think she could stay here until—" She closes her lips.

"Until what?"

With a sigh, she tells me what she had planned tonight and what ultimately stopped her.

"I can't keep her safe anymore, and I can't get away from him." She closes her eyes. "I don't know what to do."

I place my hand on her shoulder, and she opens her eyes. "I'll keep her safe, darling."

Even as the prickly feeling of my sinuses closing up overcomes me, I will absolutely keep her little cat safe. I just wish I could protect Emmy the same way.

"Are you sure?"

"I promise, and if she's here, it gives you a reason to stop by more often." I give her a wiggle of my eyebrows, and that finally pulls a smile out of her.

She notices the jacket I discarded by the door. "Where were you going?"

I shrug. I'd prefer not to admit that I was about to stalk her at my brother's house. Again.

"Food."

"Oh, I don't want to keep you. I'll get out of here so that you can get something in your belly. I guess I could . . . What? Why are you looking at me like that?"

"Are you kidding? I got plenty to eat right here." I give her a smirk as I eye her up and down. "I told you I would worship you, and while I'm not a religious man, I've always been told that the best way to worship is on your knees."

Emotions fly through her eyes—surprise, desire, desolation.

"Benji, I can't. I have to go back to him tonight." She motions to the kitten currently trying to rip open the plastic bag containing her food. "Oh shit, she's hungry. I didn't have time to give her the evening meal she's used to."

I pick up the kitten's things and start out of the room.

"Wait, what are you doing with her bed?"

I turn and walk backward so she can see me sign. "Getting her acclimated to the new house?"

I bring her kitten to the dark, quiet bedroom. Emmy sets up her things in the corner so that it looks like a regular kitty shrine. The kitten tucks in and starts enjoying her food the moment it's down, and Emmy pulls an envelope of cash from the bag. She explains that she'll need to go to the vet first thing in the morning, and that she can pay for it. I tell her to keep the money, and that I'll handle it.

"I'm sorry for asking." She strokes the cat's fur.

"Don't apologize," I sign. "I want to do this."

"Right, well, I'd better get back to him before he loses his shit even more."

We rise and leave the kitten to enjoy her food. On our way back to the living room, she notices the pile of bloody clothes on the bathroom floor. I still haven't gotten rid of them since getting in from a fucking murder last night. She starts toward them, but I stand in her way. There's no way in hell I want any of her fucking DNA on potential evidence.

"Benji, did you cut yourself again?" Her eyes go wide as she tries to peer around me.

I close the bathroom door behind me and walk her out of the bedroom without answering her. The less she knows, the safer it is for her.

She stops walking once we reach the living room, turning to look me over from the top of my head to my toes. "Are you hurt?"

I shake my head and drop onto the couch.

"That was so much blood," she says with a shudder, but she doesn't leave. She flops down beside me, takes a deep breath, and turns to face me. "Why do you cut?"

"I told you why. Trauma is a nasty bitch."

"And you can't talk about your trauma?"

My lips tighten. Aside from my family and the therapist and the monster himself, no one knows what really happened to me. I don't want sympathy or the sorrow-filled looks. Hard pass. So I just let people think I was born this way. It's easier than explaining what really happened. That someone fucked me up enough that they took my voice with them. That I shut down so hard that I never found my voice again. If the copious therapy couldn't help me discover it, I think it's gone for good.

If there were one person who could ease the grip on my vocal cords, I'd think it was her, yet we sit in pale silence.

"I don't know," I sign. "Talking about my trauma is . . . difficult."

She doesn't balk at this. She doesn't argue, either. She just rests her head on my shoulder. She smells like vanilla. I bury my face in her hair and bask in the scent.

She lifts her hand and signs something I don't expect. "I love you."

My heart thunders within my chest.

My hands rise. "My mother thought it was a medical condition. My inability to speak. One day, I talked. The next day, I didn't. She didn't know the truth until I turned seventeen. My elementary teacher, Mr. Ormsby . . ."

Now, not even my hands will work. They drop to my lap, as useless as my vocal cords.

Emmy places her hands over mine. "You don't have to say anything else," she signs.

I can't look her in the face. I don't want to see the pity there. I don't want fucking pity. I don't *deserve* pity.

"I don't cut because of what he did to me," I continue. "I cut because I'm a piece of shit who deserves to hurt."

I have stepped down from a makeshift noose in my bedroom more times than I can count because his pain infected me in ways I can't explain. It infected me and multiplied until it ate my vocal cords, devoured my heart, and left holes in my fucking brain.

Not because he touched me, but because I wasn't strong enough to stop him from touching anyone else.

"You should go," I sign. "Before Jessie gets pissed."

"Right," she says. "Are you sure you'll be okay?"

I nod. "I'll be fine. I'm gonna shower and go to bed."

Emmy looks past me, toward the bedroom. "If it's okay with you, I'd like to sit with Lily for a bit before I go. I'll lock up when I leave if you're still in the shower."

We get off the couch and head to the bedroom. I just wish it were for a different reason.

CHAPTER TWENTY-FOUR

BENJI

Hot water pelts my legs as I draw them closer to my body. I'll enjoy the heat while it lasts. I've been in here for so long that it's bound to start getting cold soon, but I'm trying to make sure Emmy is gone. The thought of facing her again after what I revealed . . . I can't.

Indescribable pain courses through my body, and I stare blankly at the shower wall as I feel all of it. Memories torture me and hold my throat closed. Not memories of the terrible things I've done in my life. Not even the memories of the murder I committed last night. It's so much worse.

These thoughts strangle me until I can't breathe. A hand clamps around my throat. It covers my mouth and digs into my cheeks, cutting off my voice. It touches me in places in absolutely shouldn't, and I can't pull away because this hand isn't mine. It's his.

Mr. Ormsby.

I'm drowning now. The pain is too real. Each thought drags across my brain like cement over raw skin. My gaze drifts higher, and I reach for the razor blade gleaming on the lower shower shelf. I rock it between my fingers and watch the way the light catches in the water droplets on the edge. The only way to end the pain is to give myself more.

So I lower the blade to my thigh. I lean back as metal spreads skin. With the rush of pain comes a release, and I finally let the tears come. They travel down my chest and mix with the crimson flooding out of me.

The thoughts quiet until only one remains. It's my voice, but it's so small and fragile. I hear the pleas of a young child. He begs. He says no. No one listens. No one hears him, but he's all I hear.

I look down at the razor again. It would be so easy. Just one swipe, and he'd finally be quiet for good. He'd learn that your voice gets you nowhere and it's better to be silent. Safer. I close my eyes and press the blade to my neck.

I'm losing my mind.

Well, what I had left of it.

But this is the way. I see that now. If I just do this, if I just drive this blade a little deeper and then pull downward, it would be over in less than a minute. The police would find the bloody clothes, and Emmy wouldn't have to—

"Benji! What the fuck are you doing?"

The blade drops from my hand and skitters across the ceramic.

Emmy rushes toward me and slams my discarded shirt over the wound. She doesn't seem to care that she's getting soaking wet, but I do. I reach up and cut off the shower.

"What did you do?" she says again as she pulls back the shirt. Blood wells within the gash and spills over the edge. Emmy shakes her head and clamps the shirt over my leg again. "We are so fucking broken, aren't we?"

She's trying to lighten the mood and add some levity to

a very heavy situation. She doesn't get it. There is no levity. There is no light.

"You shouldn't be here," I sign. "I thought you left."

"Well, I didn't. I was worried about you, and I was right to!"

I spot the bloody clothes behind her and curse myself for *still* not disposing of that shit. Everything is unraveling in front of me. "Don't forgive me."

"What? For cutting yourself?"

"Just . . . don't forgive me. Hate me if you have to."

She sits back a little. "Benji, you're scaring me."

"When you bumped into me in the hallway, I saw a look on your face that broke me because I recognized it. I've seen it in the mirror, and I will do whatever it takes to never see it on your face again. I will do whatever the fuck it takes to keep you *safe*. Do you grasp what that means? Can you fathom just how dangerous that makes me?" I look her in the eyes and point to the clothes. "You won't have to worry about him anymore."

Her hand goes to her mouth as she turns to look at the bloody rags. The pieces come together, and realization flares in her eyes.

"It doesn't matter if a guard dog is only doing what he's been bred to do. What is in his blood to do. Once he does it, he needs to be put down. I killed him, darling. To save you." I shake my head and fight off a fresh wave of tears. "See? I'm a monster, just like my brother. You should go."

But instead of running away, she moves closer. She's damn near in my lap, and if she isn't careful, she'll have a lot of explaining to do when she gets home to Jessie. I try to wrestle her off me, but she only tightens her hold.

"No," she grunts. "I'm not leaving you."

"Go," I sign. I don't want her to leave, but she *has* to!

The last thing we need is for her DNA to end up on any evidence. I push her back a bit and shove both index fingers toward her while mouthing the word. "Go!"

"No!" She leans forward and tries to kiss me, but I push her away from me.

"You have to leave. I'm not safe anymore."

"You are my *home*," she signs, speaking our language and putting so much feeling into every sign. "*You* are my safety."

She leaves no room for misinterpretation. She means what she's saying, and I don't know what to do with that. I've never been anyone's home. I've never been anyone's anything.

And now that I am, I can't be.

I lean forward and close the shower curtain, then turn on the shower again, putting an end to the discussion. Emmy lingers in the bathroom for a bit. I hear her clothes rustling, and she tries to start a few conversations, but she eventually gets the hint. The bathroom door clicks shut behind her, and I'm left alone with the scared little boy once more.

The urge to bring her back overwhelms me, the clawing need to tell her I didn't mean it, that I need her to stay, that I'm sorry. I stay silent, though. This is what's best for her, even if it's the worst possible thing for me.

CHAPTER TWENTY-FIVE

EMMY

Jessie's side of the bed is vacant when I wake up the next morning. That would normally be cause for comfort because it means he's gone to work for the day, but then the aroma of brewing coffee reaches my nose. I sit bolt upright in a panic. In the months I've lived here, Jessie has never made coffee for me in the morning. According to him, it's my duty to be up before him so that I can ensure he gets a good start to his day.

I scramble out of the bed and head for the kitchen, but I don't spot him on my way there. The kitchen is empty as well, but the scent of coffee is so strong that he couldn't have left long ago.

A sigh of relief eases out of me as I pull a coffee mug from the cabinet. He was already asleep when I returned last night, so that reward he promised never came to fruition. Thank fucking God. After leaving Benji in that state, I don't think I could have taken one more bad thing happening to me. I didn't want to leave Benji at all, but he was so adamant.

I slide the mug across the counter and pull the coffeepot from the holder.

"Morning, baby."

The pot crashes back to the holder and nearly sends coffee everywhere, but my fumbling fingers right it before disaster strikes. I spin on my heel and offer Jessie the most forced smile I can.

"Morning. Sorry I wasn't up to make your—"

"Oh, we aren't worried about that." He returns the smile, but it doesn't reach his eyes. It never reaches his eyes. And why is he hiding his hands?

"Shouldn't you be at work?"

He nods and takes a step closer, and I fight every urge to take a step back. Then his right hand appears, and my heart picks up its pace. "Want to tell me about this?"

He wiggles a small envelope—the same envelope I shoved my ill-gotten money into. When I was shoving it into a new hiding spot last night, I must have left something out of place. A cold sweat pops onto my brow.

"Oh, that? It's just some money I tucked away for Lily. She'll need to be spayed, and then there are her preventatives and annual visits." I shrug and turn back for the coffeepot. As I begin filling my cup, I do my best to pretend nothing is wrong. "I just wanted to be helpful. I never want you to feel like I'm using you."

"So you weren't planning to leave me?"

I scrunch up my nose and scoff as I pour some creamer into my mug. Even though he can't see my face, I have to keep playing the part of the unaffected woman. "Why would I want to do something like that? You're so good to me."

But as I turn around to face him again, he's revealed his other hand. This time, my heart doesn't beat faster. It stops.

"And what about these?" He cocks his head and studies the bloody clothing in his grasp. "How will you explain this away?"

"It happened at work," I blurt.

Jessie eyes me up and down. "I don't see any marks on you."

"It wasn't me. It was one of the other girls. She cut her hand really bad when she was slicing—"

"Dale is dead, Emmy. It was all over the news this morning."

The coffee mug slips from my hand and crashes to the floor.

"Hmm, is someone feeling a little guilty?"

I hurry to grab the broom to sweep up the glass. "I don't know what you're implying, Jessie."

"Baby," he coos, following my every footstep and stopping me before I get more than a few in. "You don't have to lie to me. But if you think I'm going to let you leave me?" He looks at the clothes in his hand. Enough said. "Funny, though. These aren't clothes for a woman. Whose dick have you been sucking to get them to do your dirty work?"

"I don't—" My mouth goes dry. "I didn't—"

"I just don't believe you, Emmy," he whispers against my sweat-coated forehead before pulling away and looking at me. "But I don't think you're smart enough to do something like that on your own. So tell me, who helped you?"

My lip curls. "I didn't do *anything*, Jessie." I wasn't the one who killed him.

But he can't find out who did. How would I explain why Benji would kill for me?

"Last chance, baby. Who fucking helped you?"

My lower lip trembles, and tears heat my eyes. I didn't do this! I didn't do any of it. If they test that shirt, it would be his brother's DNA all over it, not mine.

It would be Benji's DNA.

Benji.

"I did it," I whisper. "I stole the clothes from your brother so that no one would recognize me, and I—"

Fiery heat strikes my face, and my body spins to the side. I reach for the wall to keep myself upright, but there's nothing there. More pain blasts through me as I land on the floor, the wind knocked out of my lungs. Metallic liquid floods my sinuses and pours down my throat, and I can't breathe out of my nose at all. Everything is already swelling shut, and my face hurts to the point of numbness.

I blink up at Jessie as he straddles me with his legs. He drops his weight onto my abdomen and winds his hand around my throat. I'm too weak to fight him off, so I lie here and accept whatever comes next.

"How fucking dare you drag my brother into this." He spits in my face. "That was the stupidest thing you've ever done, right up there with trying to save money to leave me. You're a real bright one, aren't you?"

I scream when he fists my hair and drags my face closer to his.

"You're going to go to his apartment and apologize. Tell him what the fuck you did. He defends you all the fucking time, and I want him to know what a lying, sneaking piece of absolute trash you are. When you're done, you'll come back to me like a good little dog and take your punishment." He laughs in my face before tossing his keys onto my chest and walking away.

I lie on the kitchen floor a bit longer, too stunned to

move. Among the broken glass and spilled coffee, I feel like I'm right where I deserve to be.

My hands rise toward the ceiling. "We're so broken," I sign. My eyes close, and the tears fall.

Jessie thinks he's so smart, but he still hasn't put the final piece of the puzzle in place. What happens when he does? It won't just be the end of me, I think. No, it would be the end of all of us. And I'm the catalyst. Everything attached to me gets hurt because Jessie is too fucking insecure to make space for anyone but himself. Just look at Lily.

It's only a matter of *when* before he realizes I'm in love with Benji. We have to come up with a solution, but I think we've run out of time.

CHAPTER TWENTY-SIX

BENJI

Lying on the couch and jacking-off midmorning isn't a typical activity for me, but I can't stop thinking about what Emmy said last night. That I'm her home. That I'm her safety. It's an odd thing to get turned on by, but knowing I can be that for her, that I am who she's chosen as her protector and peace, gets me rock fucking hard.

I imagine ways things could have gone differently last night. If she hadn't had to leave, what would we have done?

That's an easy answer. I'd have—

A loud knock on the door startles me, and I release my dick. When it bangs again—louder this time, more urgent— my erection deflates in a panic, and I shove it into my pants. I'm not expecting any visitors, and the only person who would show up at my place would be Jessie or . . .

My heart shatters as I pull the door open and see her standing there. She's . . . so small. So fragile and broken. Her nose pushes toward her right eye much more than it should. Her left eye has swollen nearly shut, and her right eye is puffy at the inner corner. Dark bruising discolors her face, and dried blood crusts around her nostrils, mouth, and chin.

I don't ask what happened. I don't need to. My brother did this to her.

Before she can speak a word, I pull her into my arms and carry her to the couch. She rests her head against my chest, sobbing. Her fingers grasp my shoulders as she whispers how hopeless this is. I set her beside me on the couch.

"Jessie found the money I've been saving—" Another round of sobs steals her voice, and I stroke her head. She doesn't need to say more. If he found her stash, he knows she wants to leave him, and that's the most dangerous time for a partner in this situation. Her face is proof enough of that.

She's too upset to keep going, so I try to pull her against my chest again. She pushes back and shakes her head.

"You don't understand," she cries. "It's so much worse than that. He *knows*, Benji."

My blood is arctic air in my veins. "About us?"

"No, but how long until he figures that one out too? It's the clothes. I took them from your bathroom last night because I thought—"

"Emmy, why would you do that?" I grip her face in my hands, careful not to put pressure on the sore places.

"I took them because I thought I could help you. You've done so much for me, and I wanted to show you that I care too."

I release her face. "I know you care."

"No, I need you to know that I'll do whatever it takes for you. I want to save you, just like you want to save me."

"Can't let me be the only hero, huh?" I shake my head. I can't fuss at her. What she did was stupid, but her heart was in the right place—in my corner. "Did you tell him I did it?"

Her good eye bulges wider. "No! If he knew you killed Dale, he'd figure everything else out. Then you'd end up worse off than me. I told him I did it, and that I stole some of your clothes. That's why he hit me. He told me to come over here and apologize."

"Darling . . . I could have thought of something. I would have said I was defending *his* honor by defending *yours*. He would have believed me."

"There is no world where anyone who knew you would believe you were capable of that. You aren't like that. You aren't like *him*."

The truth of the matter is . . . I am like that.

I killed Dale.

And if I had it to do over again, I wouldn't change a thing. Anyone who hurts her deserves far worse, but I'll do what I'm capable of, and I'm capable of killing—unless it's killing my brother. As shitty as it is, I can't stop hoping that I find a solution that doesn't end with me taking his life. I don't think I can do it.

I take a closer look at Emmy's nose. "We need to get you to the hospital."

"Do you think they'll believe I walked into a door?" She points at her face. "They'll take one look at this and call the police. Jessie will flash his smile and get out of it, even if I tell them the truth, and I'll get beaten worse the next time as a thank you. Or worse, he'll try to turn in those bloody clothes, and we'll be separated by more than just a few miles and some bad decisions."

She makes a very good point.

"You'll have to do it," she says.

I shake my head. I'm not a fucking doctor. "I can't fix your face."

"Then I guess this is what you'll have to look at forever."

She tries to sniffle back a trickle of blood, but she's stopped up. She opens her mouth to get more air. This is more than just displaced.

"I don't have any pain medication," I sign. "This will be incredibly painful."

"I took some ibuprofen back at the house. I'll be fine."

My eyes widen. I hate that her being this tough in the face of adversity is turning me on. Now is not the time.

I scoot a bit closer and take the mangled bridge between my fingers. Bone scrapes against bone, but it feels like it wants to slide back home. I should know. I've fixed my own broken nose a time or two, also thanks to Jessie.

Sitting back, I give her one last chance to back out. "Are you sure you want to do this?"

"Wait, no!" she says, and I breathe an audible sigh of relief. She smacks my arm. "Not, *No, we aren't doing this.* I just need something to bite down on. Do you have a belt? I want something I can really sink my teeth into."

"Do you hear yourself?"

"Yes."

I stand and rip off my belt, which earns an adorable little sound from Emmy. Well, as adorable as it can be when her nose is blocked off. I hand it to her, and she places it between her teeth. Even in her battered state, I've never seen anything more beautiful as she looks up at me. That belt in her mouth doesn't bring my mind to the right place, so I sit on the couch and focus on her nose instead.

With my hands on her face, I'm unable to sign, so I mouth the words. *One . . . two.* I firm my grip. *Three.*

I crank to my right. Bone and cartilage scrape before clicking into place, and Emmy lets out a shrill scream as she bites the belt. A large clot falls out of her nostril and lands on my hand, but that isn't why I recoil. It's that I've caused her pain.

"I'm so sorry, darling. I'm so sorry." I lean forward and kiss her sweat-soaked forehead.

She tilts her head to the side and drops the belt from her teeth. "How does it look? Will you still love me with a crooked nose?"

"I'd love you with no nose." I kiss her forehead again and swipe the blood onto a nearby hand towel, but my smile falls as I lean back. "You can't go back to him. You have to stay here."

"I can't," she whispers. "You know that."

I pull off my shirt and hand it to her so that she can stem the trickle of blood from her nose. Then I fetch a rag and gently clean her face.

"Can't you . . . just do what you did to Dale?" she asks. She adds a small chuckle as if it were a joke. But it wasn't. She's testing the waters.

I've imagined it one million times in one million different ways since falling for Emmy. But he's my brother. My twin brother. If he and Emmy were hanging off a cliff and I had to make a choice, that would be simple, but letting someone die isn't the same as killing them. He's the only family I have left in a very isolated world. Our relationship hasn't all been bad, either. He's transformed into a monster, but I still see the person he once was.

"I can't kill my brother, but we'll figure something out. I promise. You can't go back to him tonight, though."

"It's not like that. I'm not going back to him out of choice. If I could choose, it would be you. I'm yours, Benji. I may fall asleep beside your brother every night, but my every waking thought revolves around you."

"Then if you can't stay, let me make you mine before you go." I stand and lead her to the bedroom.

I wasn't lying when I said I'd love her with or without a nose. Even with her face in its current state, I've never seen a more beautiful woman. And as I ease off her shirt, I see so much more to admire. I remove clothing until every stunning inch is laid bare before me, and then I strip as well. I lay her on the bed and crawl between her legs. Every ounce of anguish she's experienced tonight must be replaced by intense pleasure, and I'm the man to give her all of it.

The moment my mouth meets her pussy, my dick throbs against the mattress. I lick and lap at her, pushing two fingers inside her. She writhes and grips the sheets, her pain forgotten. My dick pulses. I may be enjoying every second between her thighs, but I'm doing this for her. I'm replacing that pain with something so much better.

Because this is what we have. It isn't much, but this moment, all these little moments with her? They make my world turn, and if anyone tries to stop it from turning, I'll burn the son of a bitch to ash. I'm spinning on a tight axis, spiraling out of orbit as I inch her closer to bliss, and each sound that eases out of her brings me closer to my own release.

It's too much to bear when she comes around my fingers. Without even touching my cock, I join her. My hand barely gets between my legs to catch the mess as it jets out of me, but I don't want to waste it. Also, it's a little embarrassing that I keep coming from eating her out, but her pleasure is so intimately connected to my own.

I take every drop into my mouth. Then I grip the insides of her thighs and pull her flush against my face as I fuck her with my tongue, pushing my come inside her. I paint her walls with it, marking her before I've even fucked her.

I rub my hand along my spent cock, willing him to wake the fuck up. I'm not finished yet. I get to my knees, flip her around, and pull her ass against my crotch, and it's all the encouragement I need.

Hard once more, I push inside her and grip her hips. She looks at me over her shoulder, moaning through each frenzied thrust. She's already close again, and I've only gotten started.

The piercings rake her opening, and I lean back to look at what I'm doing to her. That's when I realize that the force has also broken open the gash on my thigh. Blood trails down my leg, and I scoop a bit onto my fingers. On her lower back, I paint a letter with each forceful thrust.

M-I-N-E . . . because that's what she is. She's fucking mine. She doesn't know it, but I'd lay down my life for her. I'd give up the right to breathe to offer her the gift of freedom. But I'm selfish because I don't want this to end yet. I would die for her, and at the end of all of this, that might be what I have coming, but for right now, I will live to fight for her.

WE LIE IN THE BED, wrapped in each other's arms as if we have the right. Jessie texted Emmy to let her know he wouldn't be home after work, so she asked for permission to stay at my place for the day so that she could play with her cat. We've definitely been playing with her cat, just not the one Jessie believes. Surprisingly, he told her not to come back until after midnight. He said he was having some of the "boys" over, which is probably code for other women.

Emmy knows this, but she no longer cares if he's faithful. She hasn't for some time. After what we've been doing off and on all day, she doesn't really have a right. Even so, midnight is fast approaching, and she still plans to go back to him. I've begged her to stay, but she refuses.

A tear slips down her cheek, and my heart shatters. "What's wrong?"

"Nothing," she whispers, shaking her head to hide her tears. "Everything."

I put my hands on either side of her face and draw her toward me. Her mouth is so close to mine that I can smell the scent of her salty tears cresting the most perfect lips I've ever seen.

"I love you so fucking much," she finally says, and her exhale sends the physical signs of her sadness against my lips. "And I can't. We can't be more than this."

I kiss her, tasting that sadness. The hurt that I'm causing by selfishly loving her.

"No," I sign, "I will not let you go. Just stay with me tonight. We'll think of an excuse."

"I can't."

I know.

I lean her head on my shoulder, and we bask in what little time we have left. Emmy exhales and looks up at me. Her eyes fixate on my neck.

"What's the semicolon for?"

My breath catches. I've never been ashamed of this tattoo, but it's not something I've wanted to talk about. Maybe it's my anti-social personality or my lack of voice, but no one has ever asked me about it, and I liked it that way. I had hoped the symbolism would be enough.

"A period ends a sentence. A semicolon lets you know that there is more to say."

"You mean . . ."

"Yeah, I've had a few attempts. After the last one, I decided I wasn't done writing my story, so I got the semicolon."

"Death seems like a fitting solution to everything we're going through," she whispers.

I shake my head and bring her hand to my inner arm, along another thin scar she might not have noticed before now. Then to my abdomen, and finally my neck.

"It took a long time to stop wanting to die. To stop feeling like I had nothing to live for. I found the will to keep going before I met you, darling, but you showed me that I haven't been living. Now . . . I want to."

"How can you keep going when everything seems so hopeless?"

"You. I keep going for you. If you go, I'm going with you, and who would stop me? You'd be—"

"Benji, don't talk like that."

"Why not? I'm just repeating your own shit back to you. Just remember that I'm your shadow. I'm attached to you, even in death. Maybe more so. If you go, I go with you." I place my hand over her heart, then sign, "If you don't want to be with me, don't, but ending your life won't break our bond. Wherever you go after this, I'll follow. I will trail you all the way to hell if I have to, darling. I'll burn with you."

"There has to be a way this works out for us. There has to be."

"If there is, we'll find it. Just don't give up, yeah?" I tap my neck. "Semicolon . . . we've got so much more to say."

"I love you," she signs.

I love her too. More than words can express, so I don't use any. I pull her over my body, and for the final time tonight, I prepare to worship her. Midnight is fast approaching, but it isn't here yet.

CHAPTER TWENTY-SEVEN

Sunlight streams over my face, and I snuggle closer to Benji's chest. My eyelashes flutter open. I stretch my hand over bare skin and sigh deeply. Never did I think I'd get to wake up beside . . .

Wake up? Sunlight?

"Shit! Benji, get up!" I toss the covers off him, revealing his naked body. Memories of last night crash into me. We said one more . . . and then we fell asleep. I hop off the bed and start searching for my clothes. "Fuck, fuck, fuck. Does he have a key to this place? Could he have seen us?"

Benji is already on his feet, pulling on clothes and looking around the room for mine. He hands my shirt to me. "He wouldn't have just looked if he'd walked in on that."

Good point.

Still, he's probably not very happy with me for staying out all night, and Benji knows it. Even as he kneels before me and starts tying my sneaker, he doesn't want me to go.

"I don't think you should go back," he signs when he's done up the laces. "Stay with me. I'll protect you from him."

"I have to go back," I say.

What I don't say is that I spent all yesterday thinking up a plan of my own. If I told him what I'm about to do, he'd never agree to it, so I keep it to myself. There's just one piece of the equation that concerns me.

"Can you do something for me?" I ask.

"Anything."

"If you don't hear from me by five—"

"No." He shakes his head. "Darling . . . no."

The gravity of what I'm saying crosses his features, and the handsome, broken man I've fallen for becomes a child in front of my eyes. I've never seen someone look so fucking scared.

"Promise me."

"Stay with me. We both suck at keeping promises."

"Five p.m., okay?" I lean forward and kiss him. "Not a second sooner. Or later."

"I'm coming with you," he signs as he follows me to the door. "I can't lose you."

Though I wish he could come with me, though I wish I could draw from his strength, there are some things we must do on our own.

"I love you," I sign. "Five?"

He drops his hands and gives me a single nod, then kisses me again before I head for the car.

It's almost eight in the morning, so Jessie has surely left for work by now. That's perfect. It gives me time to set things up and get my ducks in a row before he comes home at four. As soon as it's done, I'll call Benji and tell him. Then it will be my turn to deny forgiveness.

Because Benji can't bring himself to kill his brother. But maybe I can.

I speed past familiar streets and places until I reach his dreaded home. The driveway and garage are empty when I pull closer to the house. Part one of my plan has gone well, then. I look around before slamming the car door closed behind me. Jessie's house is set so far back from the road that no one should hear his cries for help. They certainly never heard mine.

Now I just have to figure out how to do this.

I hurry into the house and head straight for the safe, but that's a terrible idea. The neighbors might not hear screaming, but a gunshot would carry to the next county. I'm too small to overpower him, but maybe I could stab him. Poison would be too premeditated. I need this to look like an altercation gone wrong.

Or right, in my case.

I also need to find the money and those bloody clothes. Maybe I should—

"Welcome home, baby."

My heart hammers as I spin on my heel and find him standing behind me in the hallway. His hair is a mess, and he looks like he hasn't slept a wink. He even missed a few buttons on his shirt.

"Jessie," I squeak out. "What are you doing here? Shouldn't you be at work?"

He takes a step closer, and I press my back against the hallway wall. "I had a surprise for you, Emmy. Last night, it was all set up, and I waited for you. You never came."

"My face was so swollen. I couldn't see well enough to drive in the dark."

"Oh." He takes another step toward me. "I'm ready to give it to you now."

"Stay back," I whisper. "I don't want anything from you. This is over, Jessie."

He stops. At first he looks hurt. His chin quivers, and his eyes fill with tears. But the sadness fades as maniacal laughter fills the silence. "Since when do you have a spine?"

As he charges forward, I'm out of options. I reach for the decorative shelf above my head and rip it off the wall. With a feral scream, I swing it toward him and strike the side of his head. He stumbles against the wall, then regains his footing and grabs my hair.

"Your actions have consequences, baby. Every fucking one of them!"

My forehead collides with drywall, and I'm stunned into silence as he snatches my head back again and throws me to the floor. With a growl, he flips me onto my back and sits on my chest. Blood trickles down the side of his face from the fresh wound in his scalp. But he isn't finished with me. He firms his grip in my hair and slams the back of my head into the hardwood floor.

"You aren't leaving me," he snarls into my face. "You are mine! *Mine!*"

"I don't love you!"

"You don't need to love me," he growls, "but you will *not* leave me."

I bring my knee as high as I can when he goes to stand, and I catch him in the nuts. He bends at the waist and leans against the wall, giving me just enough space to slither out from under him. My legs are useless as I rush down the hall-way. It feels like running through water. Before I can reach the living room, his hand clamps around my arm and snatches me backward.

Gripping my shoulders, Jessie throws me against the wall. Picture frames crash to the floor, scattering glass beneath our feet. His hands wrap around my throat and tighten. I reach up and claw his fingers and wrists until several of my nails snap backward, but it's no use. He's too strong. He just grits his teeth and tightens his hold.

I kick and fight until my body betrays me. I fight until I know I can't win. As the blackness encroaches on my vision, I stop fighting. I think of Benji. He didn't want me to leave. He trusted that I could figure this out on my own. He won't try to reach me for hours, and by then, I'll be long gone.

"If I can't be with you, you can't exist," Jessie whispers. At least . . . it sounds like a whisper. His voice is so far away, and I can't see anything anymore. "Do you understand that? I will kill you before I subject myself to a world where I don't own you."

I'm unable to speak, so I raise my hands in a defiant last attempt to be heard. "Fuck you," I sign. If those are my final words, then so be it, but they needed to be said. I needed to say *something*.

And the world goes black.

A DEEP PAIN pulses at the back of my skull. I'm too tired to open my eyes, and they hurt too. My body feels like lead, and my neck . . . What the fuck? I reach up and nearly scream when my fingers collide with metal. I sit up, but a chain snatches me backward. I'm secured to the fucking wall.

"Do you like it, baby? I worked hard last night, setting this up just for you." Jessie rises from a chair in the corner of his bedroom. "I didn't want to do this. You know that, right?"

My eyes struggle to adjust to the dim light in the room, but I'm less concerned by what I see and much, *much* more concerned by what I smell. Is that . . . gasoline?

"Jessie, what are you doing?"

Do I need to ask? Isn't it apparent? I'm chained to the wall, and the scent of gas is so strong in here that I might vomit. He plans to set me on fucking fire.

He sits on the edge of the bed and looks at me like he feels sorry for me. "You shouldn't have tried to leave me. I *told* you what would happen if you did. Do you remember when I told you that?"

He's talking to me like I'm a child. He's talking to me like a pet he fucking owns.

"You don't have to do this," I plead. "We could talk about it."

His eyes widen, and he gets to his feet again. "You did this! You! There is nothing more to talk about. I found the money. You didn't run to the cops after I put you in your place yesterday, but I bet Benji stopped you. He did, didn't he?" He runs his hands through his hair, eyes wild. "It's only a matter of time before you leave. You can't. You won't leave me."

His eyes rush to mine—such familiar eyes. His brother's are the same shape, the same color. But they aren't the same. Possession resides within both of their longing glances, but the source of that possession couldn't be more different. Benji wants to cherish me, care for me and watch me flourish. Jessie wants to keep me hidden in a cage where he can poke me as he pleases. Or turn me to ashes. Whatever mood he's in that day.

He starts to pace. "I'm really doing you a favor. Would you rather be dead or in prison?"

Probably prison. But I don't answer him.

"I'm showing you a final kindness," he says. "I'm euthanizing you. Like a sick little dog, you need to be put down."

He mutters something else as he reaches into his pocket. When he produces a tiny glass vial and holds it to his nose, I'm not surprised. I've long suspected something more than alcohol spurred on his rage, and now I know I was correct. He takes a long sniff and tips his head back.

"I'm not letting you go alone, though. We'll take this journey together, baby."

"What do you mean?" My heart hammers harder. "You have too much to live for, Jessie. Don't do this. Benji needs you!"

"Benji?" He scoffs and throws the vial against the wall. "I am so sick of taking care of him. Ever since that teacher touched him a little, he's been a fucking problem." Jessie closes his lips with a smirk. "Whoops. Wasn't supposed to let Benji's dirty little secret out of the bag."

"You're sick," I whisper.

He turns with a shout and rams his fist through the wall. I scream and try to scramble away, but the chain is so short. It pulls taut and snatches me backward by my neck.

"You're such a fucking *bitch!* I gave you everything. Paid off your lease. Bought you anything you asked for! You couldn't just *love* me? Or fucking *pretend* to?"

I look at the clock beside me. I can't keep him going until after five. Not with the way he looks. The way he sounds. It's just after two, and I don't have hours left to live. I don't even know if I have minutes.

Especially not once he lifts that red gas can and stomps to the other side of the room. He starts dousing the curtains, then the floor by the window, ensuring we can't escape. He continues to the dresser, drenching the wood and the floor beneath it. I cough as the strong fumes invade my lungs, but

I'm relieved when he tips the can over the bed and nothing comes out. He's out of fuel.

The can lands on the floor with a hollow clatter. "You ruined my life. You took away the one thing I wanted to live for . . . *you*."

"Please, Jessie. Please don't do this," I plead as he reaches into his pocket.

He eases a Zippo from the shadows and fingers the wheel. Tiny sparks fly from the flint with each strike, and any of them would be enough to send us straight to hell. He didn't soak the bed in gas, but he doesn't need to. Once this fire gets going, it will devour everything in its path, gasoline or not.

"Think about what you're doing!" I yell. "This doesn't solve anything. You could have any woman you want. You don't need me."

Jessie smiles at me, and it's the most unnerving thing I've ever seen. It tells me he does. At least, in his mind he does.

His thumb blazes over the wheel, once, twice. The flame erupts from the lighter and balances on the metal. A moment of indecision flashes through his eyes, but it passes just as quickly. He stares into the flame and shakes his head.

"I've chosen a good end for us. Fire is the great purifier."

"It will hurt," I say, gripping that glimpse of fear I saw in his face as he first held that flame. "You've been burned before. You know what this will feel like."

"A momentary ache to snuff out the torment of our lives." He scoffs and shakes his head. "Once the nerve endings burn away, we'll feel nothing. And then we'll be nothing." He faces me. "Together."

I sob as he balances the lighter between two fingers. Then I close my eyes and accept that this is how it ends.

CHAPTER TWENTY-EIGHT

BENJI

I promised her I'd wait until five, but it's yet another promise that I just can't keep. Each minute without her felt like years slipping through my fingers. Whatever she planned, it was stupid of me to let her go through it alone.

I nearly put the car on two wheels as I take the turn onto Jessie's street. This feeling has been clawing at me for the past three hours, growing hotter and tighter and more cloying. The only thing that will end the torment is to see her. Once I know she's alive and well, I'll just slink back to my place.

Both vehicles are in the driveway when I pull up, but that isn't what makes me feel sick. It's that the door to the shed has been left wide open. Jessie keeps all of his yard-work shit in there, but he hires a guy to do the actual work. The guy isn't due out for a few weeks, so that shed shouldn't be open.

Bile rises up my throat. I don't think I can forgive myself

if something happens to Emmy because of me, even though it kind of already has.

I rush onto the porch and stop in front of the door. My hand grips the handle. I don't listen to my gut often, but I listen to it now as I push inside. It's screaming at me, telling me something is very wrong.

The acrid scent of gasoline drifts on the air-conditioned breeze as I step over the threshold. Jessie's muffled shouts reach me from deeper inside the house, so I head toward them.

Pictures lie in a mess of broken glass in the hallway. I step over them, careful not to alert my brother to my presence as I creep closer. The sound of his voice grows, as does the scent of gasoline. Emmy says something, but it's too quiet to make out. Jessie hears it, though, because he starts screaming at her again.

When I finally reach the doorway to his bedroom, I can't believe my eyes. Emmy is chained to the wall via a metal collar around her neck. She looks exhausted. Her face is pale, and the bruises stand out even darker against her skin. Jessie stands over her, screaming into her face as his right hand moves a lit lighter around.

A lighter.

Gasoline.

"You said you loved me! Isn't this what love is?" He moves the flame between them. "We go together, Emmy."

I open my mouth to scream at him, to yell for him to stop, but nothing comes out. I will my vocal cords to work, just this once. Rushing him right now all but guarantees he'll drop that lighter into gasoline. I need to talk to him, but the sound remains buried in my fucking throat. Hell, even if I could yell for him, he'd probably still set them ablaze.

Emmy hasn't noticed me standing here. Her frantic

gaze transfixes on the flame near her head, and she opens her mouth in unintelligible wails as he continues berating her with his voice. I can't watch another second of this. It's killing me.

I know my brother. I know what's about to happen. In a last desperate attempt to save us all, I ball up my voice and visualize throwing up one word. That's what the therapist taught me to do, and I tried for years, but it never worked. She said I needed to visualize. Well, I'm fucking visualizing.

My throat tightens and chokes me. I can't even get air, but I keep trying. I will the word forward.

"S-stop." The word spills from me, but it's too quiet to be heard over Jessie's shouting and Emmy's crying. I close my eyes and imagine throwing the word this time. "*Stop!*"

Silence descends as Jessie's head whips toward me. Emmy closes her eyes and opens her mouth in a silent sob.

"Don't do this," I sign, too afraid to try speaking again.

"Now you decide to talk? *Now?*" He looks from me to the lighter. "I'm sorry, little brother. It's too late. It's already done."

He tosses the lighter, and the far wall erupts in a blinding flash of light. The curtains become molten lava in seconds, dripping down the wall, and as the flames follow the path of gasoline, they devour the dresser and wash us in a fiery heat. We maybe have five minutes before the blaze blocks our exit.

I charge forward and spear Jessie to the floor. Today is the day he learns that he has never beaten me. He's been handed every victory. This time, I won't hold back. He collides with a thud and a rush of air, but I don't give him time to catch his breath. My fists fly into his face, bashing him until he's on the brink of consciousness. He can't even get his hands between us to defend himself. His eyes roll back, and I land a final blow to his jaw before he goes completely slack.

As Emmy screams, I tear my eyes away from my brother and look at the flames. They're licking closer and closer to the bed, but that isn't where she's looking. I follow her gaze to the ceiling, which looks like something out of a horror film. Burning light flickers and creeps ever closer—as above, so below.

"Hurry, Benji!" she screams.

I dig through Jessie's pockets and find a key ring. The key I need has to be here. Gripping it tightly to my chest, I rush for the bed. My fingers shake as I try the first key, but it doesn't fit. I swap to the next one, but it's another dud. On the third try, I drop the fucking key ring.

"Hey," Emmy says, and I look at her. "I love you, Benji." Her eyes close. "You have to get out. Once that ceiling goes—"

"I love y-you," I say. I can't say the rest. That I won't leave her. That if she has to die in this inferno, then so do I. Those three stammered words have to say everything I can't because there isn't enough time.

Her eyes open, and she nods. She understands. We make it out of this together . . . or we don't.

I grab the keys and try two more, but of course the correct key is the last one on the ring. After a few more tense seconds, she's free. Her arms wind around my neck, and I raise her into my arms. But as I spin to get her out of here, Jessie blocks our path, standing just in front of the doorway.

Blood pours from his right ear and a gash below his left ear. His head cocks to the side as he studies me clutching Emmy to my chest. "What's this?"

I grip her tighter, and she cries into my shirt.

"Put her down, Benji," he says. "She stays with me until the end."

I shake my head. With my arms wrapped around her, it's impossible to sign, and speaking isn't exactly easy.

"Let us go, Jessie," Emmy pleads. "It's over!"

"No! You don't get to leave me!"

The ceiling groans overhead as the flames eat through beams. Smoke chokes off the light so that only the fire casts a ghastly glow over our faces. But that isn't the only thing choking. Emmy starts to cough in my arms, and I have to get her out of here.

Jessie takes a step toward us as a beam breaks loose overhead. It crashes on top of him, knocking him out . . . and barring our exit. The fiery wooden structure lies directly in front of the threshold.

I look from my brother to Emmy.

"No," she says, but a hacking cough steals her voice.

She already knows what I'm thinking.

I step closer to the beam, and heat rushes forward to singe my skin. Emmy's grip tightens on my shirt as she claws and struggles to keep her hold on me. My lips meet hers, and she stills.

"I love you," I whisper against her mouth.

And then I throw her through a wall of flames.

CHAPTER TWENTY-NINE

EMMY

"Benji, no!" I run toward the fire, but my body works against me. The moment I feel the heat against my skin, I stop walking forward and shield my face. It's so much hotter than it was two seconds ago, and the fire is only growing. Smoke curls out of the room, obscuring my view. I listen for the sounds of their voices, for the sounds of a scuffle . . . anything!

But only the crackle of fire consuming everything greets my ears.

I cough and try to force my way through the heat again, but my body refuses. I drop to my knees and scream. Not Benji. He deserved better than this. Better than me. He deserved the world, and now he'll die a fiery death.

Because of me.

Now I suddenly realize Jessie's desperation. The thought of living the rest of my life without the person I love is something I don't think I can stomach. This loss claws within me, eating me alive and doing more damage than the fire could do to my physical being. There is no end to this pain.

I take a step backward as more smoke pours out of the room. Something collapses with a crash inside, and I stare at that doorway, willing Benji to emerge. He doesn't, and I'm out of time. If I don't leave right now, I'll die here too.

I drop to my knees. Maybe it's better this way.

But as I look up again, a figure bursts through the haze. It's Benji, and he has his brother's unconscious form in his arms. He stumbles to a stop and drops Jessie to the floor as the blaze crackles behind him. Heaving, he leans against the wall and nearly collapses.

"Why?" I ask as I look from him to his brother. "After all he's done, why would you save him?"

But then he reaches into his pocket and produces a knife. He isn't trying to save his twin. He's trying to give me the gift of retribution.

He pushes the knife toward me, but I'm thinking ahead a few steps. I shake my head and push it back to him. Jessie will die, but it won't be by either of our hands. Instead, I pull Benji into me and kiss him.

"I'm sorry I didn't keep our promise," he says. He stumbles over a few words, but that's to be expected.

"Thank God you didn't."

"We should get out of here." He grunts and raises his hands to sign the rest. "This house will come down around us."

I look down at Jessie. He's starting to come to, and that doesn't bode well for my plan. I figured the smoke inhalation would take him out and keep our hands clean, but that isn't looking like an option anymore.

He blinks up at us, then looks at the flames just a few

feet away. "My legs," he says past a busted lip. "I can't feel anything from the waist down! Get me out of here!"

"The beam," I whisper.

Benji nods. "Paralyzed him."

"Drag him down the hall a bit," I say, and they both give me a look. "Just far enough from the fire that you and I are safe."

Realizing what I have planned, Benji grabs his brother beneath the arms and pulls him further down the hallway. It doesn't buy much time, but it's enough. Unfortunately, Jessie tries to pull himself closer to the exit, and I can't have that. I kick the heavy hallway table over his legs, preventing him from dragging himself any further.

"You don't have to do this!" Jessie pleads.

"Funny," I say as I yank off my shorts. "I remember saying the same thing."

"What are you doing?" He licks his lips and tries to heave the table off his lap, but without his lower half to support him, he just flops around. "Stop undressing and help me!"

Benji drops to his knees in front of me. He looks up at me with familiar eyes. These eyes are kind, and they say they'll worship me, even among the flames. Even until his dying breath.

"Don't you dare!" Jessie screams. "She's mine, Benji! After all I've done for you, this is how you repay your brother? Don't do it! She's mine! *Mine!*"

I spare Jessie a final glance. "You're wrong, Jessie. I've been Benji's from the start. I just took too long to realize it."

"Mine," Benji growls.

He lowers my panties and presses his mouth to my pussy. As his tongue finds that secret place that makes my toes curl, Jessie's screams of rage provide a symphonic accompaniment.

"Fuck me in front of him so he can think of this as he dies," I say.

Benji pulls back and raises an eyebrow.

I took it too far. I definitely took it too far. That was a little too much. I don't know what's gotten into—

"Anything for you, darling," he signs, and my chest flutters.

It should be illegal to love a man this much, but as he spins me to face him and pins me against the wall, my feelings for him damn near cause me to explode.

He smirks, and his piercings graze my mouth. "Mine."

"Yours," I pant.

He pushes inside me as our mouths meet. I look away from Jessie, focusing instead on the encroaching flames. Sweat soaks our bodies, and the heat is almost too much to bear. But if the threat of Jessie wasn't enough to stop us, a little fire certainly doesn't stand a chance.

"You are mine to cherish, to use, to fill," Benji says. His voice shakes, but his words are sure. "You will never know pleasure again unless it's from my hand. Just keep taking care of me this well, and I'll shelter you from any storm. Just keep being the woman of my dreams, my darling Emmy."

Benji pulls out of me and picks me up. I wrap my legs around his waist and slide him inside me. With one hand around his neck, I bring the other between my legs. I want Jessie to see how good Benji makes me feel. He needs to know what it sounds like when I actually come.

As he brings me closer to detonation, he looks into my eyes. The fire and smoke disappear, and we're all that's left.

"I feel you," he whispers. "You're so close. Come for me."

I tip my head back and come.

"You're mine, and I will never let you go."

Heat fills me as he finishes inside me, and as the high fades, we both realize the level of danger we're in. Smoke fills the hallway, and the walls have caught fire. We hurry to get our clothes on and nearly trip over Jessie's immobile legs in the process.

"You sure you're okay with leaving your boyfriend to die in a painful fire?" Benji signs as we prepare to leave.

I look down at Jessie, who continues to beg for our help, though his pleas are mere whispers now. "Oh, that guy? He's my ex."

We step over his legs and leave the fire to clean up our mess. We have a life to rebuild.

CHAPTER THIRTY

BENJI

The firetrucks arrived in a rush of sound and light, but it was too late to save the house. Or my brother. Emmy and I came up with a story about how Jessie lost it, killed Dale, and then tried to burn the house down. The evidence of our crimes burned with him. We'll have to endure the evidence of Jessie's and Dale's and Mr. Ormsby's crimes for the rest of our lives, though.

We don't know if the police bought it. They said we'd have to come in for more questions, just until their investigation was completed. They said we shouldn't skip town. But they let us go for now, and we made the short trip across town to my apartment.

Emmy reclines on the couch with an ice pack pressed against her face. It's still swollen and sore and terribly bruised. The paramedics wanted us to go with them, citing something about the danger of smoke inhalation, but Emmy and I both knew what we needed to start healing.

Each other.

We've been trying to heal for months, and now that the splinters and debris have been removed from our gaping wounds, maybe we can. Well . . . most of the debris has been removed. There is still one man who should pay for what he did to a terrified little boy all those years ago, but he probably never will. Hell, he's probably long dead by now, which is even more depressing. He should suffer.

Emmy pats the couch, urging me to come sit with her. I do as she asks, sliding in under her head so I can hold the ice pack for her. She lets out a contented sigh, and I'm inclined to do the same. We did it. We're finally free.

"How does it feel to have your voice back?" she asks.

I raise my hands to respond, but then I lower them. "Weird," I say.

"If you want to keep signing, you should. For once in your life, do what makes Benji happy."

"Thank you, darling," I sign.

"You're welcome, my love," she signs back.

My love.

She doesn't just belong to me. I'm hers as well. I am her lover, her protector. I am her safe space and her confidant. But more than anything, I am her *home.*

The cat jumps onto her stomach, and Emmy reaches out to stroke her fur. "Oh shit! Were you able to take Lily to the vet?"

I nod. "The tail is broken, but it will heal on its own. They gave her some pain meds and said you overfeed her."

"I do not."

I smile to myself. She so does.

Never in my wildest imaginings did I think this is where I would be right now—at home with the love of my life as we laugh at the antics of a walking allergy attack. The last twin standing. The man who reached for what he wanted and took it.

"I love you," I say, and Emmy smiles.

"I never thought I'd hear your voice. I still can't believe it."

"I never thought I'd hear it either." I clear my throat, but it still feels wrong to speak, so I raise my hands. "Sounds a little different from when I was a kid."

Emmy laughs. "I'd imagine so."

"So what do we do now?"

"With Dale dead, I don't know what that means for our jobs. I suppose we need to get out there and find some work."

"What about your real estate license?"

"About that . . . I might have told a little fib to impress you guys in the beginning. I'm not a real estate agent. Just a lowly bar whore." She winces and peers up at me. "Does that change how you feel about me?"

I brush the hair out of her face so that she can see me clearly. My response is more than my fragile, unworked vocal cords can handle. "Nothing will ever change the way I feel. Not time or distance. Not even family or the threat of death will degrade the emotions. What I feel for you is endless and eternal. It's stronger than the tide. I tried to fight it, but it's a force greater than anything I've experienced, and I don't want to push against it anymore. I want it to carry me to you, because I am your home, and darling, you are *mine*. I promise you that."

She pulls the ice pack off her face and sits up to face me. "When you speak to me, I hear you. I trust you. Is this a promise you'll keep?"

I pull her into me and kiss her. Yes. This is one promise I will die to keep, and I've proven that. I will love this woman until my dying breath, and if whatever waits beyond permits it, I'll love her then too. If they won't permit it, I'll fight the omniscience until it relents. This is the love of a lifetime. It's the love of one-thousand lifetimes, and I will find her in each of them.

Easing away from the kiss, I flash Emmy a sly smirk. "It's almost time for Lily's pain meds. What do you say we go do a little pain management of our own after we've taken care of her?"

"Shouldn't we go over the story for the cops a few more times?"

"Tell you what . . . you can recite the story while I'm eating that perfect little pussy, and each time you get it right, I'll let you come on my tongue."

She bites her lip. "Practice makes perfect, right?"

I nod.

With a giggle, she hurries toward the bedroom, already stripping off her shirt. I didn't know how long it would take her to smile after the hell she's been through, but I'm glad to see she's still my ray of sunshine in a storm. Jessie didn't break her spirit, and now I can ensure no one ever does.

Giving medication to a cat isn't the easiest task, but I get it done and hurry to the bedroom. The pussy I really want to mess with is calling my name.

Emmy lies back on the comforter, completely nude. Despite a shower, soot still darkens her nostrils, and the swelling and bruising on her face distort her features. More bruising colors her body in places it shouldn't. In shapes it shouldn't.

Yet I've never seen anything more beautiful.

I am a man blinded by love, and I hope I never see again. If she gains weight, I don't care. If she ages like a banana and goes gray and wrinkled in five years, I give zero fucks. Because she is mine and I am hers, and until the day I die, that's just the way it's going to be. Not because I'll make her stay the way my brother did, but because for the two of us, there is no one else.

Because she has been my obsession, my goddess, since the moment I saw her. I have kneeled at her feet, and she has raised me from ash. As I gaze at her perfection now, I can say that the Bible got one thing right. Her body is definitely a temple, and I need to go worship.

EPILOGUE

Benji

It's been several months since Jessie's house burned to the ground with him in it. We anticipated lots of questions. We received very few. The police took our statements several times, and we both talked about how we tried to get Jessie out. He just kept running back in for one more thing . . .

The cops bought it, as did the insurance company. The paralysis bit certainly helped sell the story. So did the fact that they found just enough of some scorched, bloodstained clothing to pull Dale's DNA from it. There was also my DNA, but because Jessie and I are identical twins, it's an identical match for most early forensic testing. Emmy spun it so that they believed Jessie killed Dale in a jealous rage, and this brilliant woman had the scathing texts from Jessie to back it up. That was enough for them. The police were happy to close the case quickly without pushing for more complete forensic testing that would have excluded him and shined a nasty spotlight on me.

With the insurance payout from Jessie's complete loss of life and property, Emmy and I are set up to take it easy for a bit, though she's still looking for work. Her prior felony conviction didn't disappear in the fire, after all. Thankfully, her supervising officer has been understanding with everything that's happened, and she's been shown a lot of leniency.

Despite regaining the use of my voice, I still choose to sign. It's nice to have a way to communicate with Emmy that most people don't understand. It's also been nice to go out in public with her without fear of my brother chasing us down. That's a fear we'll never have to worry about again.

The bell above the diner door rings, and out of habit, I look back to see who came in. My hand falls from hers and my mouth goes dry.

"What's the matter?" Emmy asks.

I can't even answer her, because standing not ten feet away is the man who stole my voice and almost stole my life. He even wore the same cap back then—a gray wool thing that pushes his hair onto his ears. I can't look at him for more than a second before I'm standing up and running out of the diner. Not because I'm afraid of him, but because I'm afraid of what I'll fucking do to him if I don't get out of here.

Emmy trails behind me, trying to keep up with a man in a full-blown rage. Once we're outside, she grabs my arm and spins me around. "You have your voice now, Benji."

"What does that have to do with anything?" I take a step back. "Each time he hurt me, I wanted to yell. Each time he touched me, I wanted to tell someone. He silenced me."

She blinks at me. "You don't have to be silent anymore. You saved me from my abuser, and now it's my turn to save you."

"You set this up?" I shake my head and turn away. "It's over. It doesn't matter anymore."

Her eyes narrow on me before she points at my thighs. "That man still does that to you." Her finger grazes the tattoo on my neck. "He did this to you." Her hand wraps around my wrist. "He tried to take your life, Benji."

And he almost succeeded.

The diner door slams, and we pin ourselves against the building as he takes off down the street at a quick clip. He glances around, but he doesn't notice us.

"He thought he was meeting a little boy here," Emmy whispers. "I guess something spooked him."

Without another word, I nod at her, and we follow him. We stay just out of sight until we reach a small house on the outskirts of the city. I don't know how I imagined him living, but part of me is pleased to see that it looks like shit. Weeds overtake the yard, and vines cover the eaves. I guess being a pervert has a way of isolating him as much as it isolates his victims. How kind of him to share this little gift with us.

And I say *us* because I know there were more. I couldn't have been the only one he hurt. That's what crushes me. Who did he abuse after he was finished with me? Who did he fuck up because I was too fucked up to relive those memories in court?

It takes everything in me to keep my feet moving toward a man I instinctively want to run from, but Emmy gives me the strength to keep going forward. We sneak behind him as he's unlocking the door, and the moment the lock disengages and the knob turns, we rush in behind him and push him inside. His wide eyes look around as his body slams against a wall. When his watery gaze focuses on me, I can't tell if he recognizes me. I'm a lot bigger now. I look a lot different now too. Years of mental anguish will do that to you.

"Grab a chair," I say, and Emmy drags a kitchen chair into the living room and plops it down on the dingy carpet.

"Take whatever money I have in my wallet, just please don't hurt me!" he whines as I set him down on the chair.

I turn to Emmy as I hold down his writhing body. "Any tape, rope, or chains lying around? Time to make Mr. Ormsby here a little less comfortable."

Emmy disappears again and reappears with a roll of duct tape.

"Good girl," I say as I take it from her.

Only once he's firmly secured do I toss the tape to the floor and draw back to look at him. There are more wrinkles on this face than the one that haunts my nightmares, but it's him. Does he recognize me yet? Doesn't seem so with the way he's blabbering and screaming about money and watches. I don't want his money. I don't want his things. I want the years he stole from me.

Since I can't get that, I'll just have to rob him of the rest of his.

"Hey, teach," I say as his scared eyes settle on my face.

"Wh-who are you?"

"Do you remember the sweet little boy with the dinosaur backpack and matching lunchbox? I know you remember it because you complimented me on it every time. Just before you'd pick me up and put me on your desk. Do you remember that? I sure as fuck do. I relive it every single time I close my eyes."

"Benji Rinehart."

I smile and lean closer to him. "The one and only. Do you know what you did to me? You took so much from me.

My innocence. My fucking *voice*. Do you remember the last word I ever spoke to you?"

He shakes his head, sending his shitty gray cap to the floor.

"*Stop*. That was the last thing I said." I turn to face Emmy. "And thanks to her, it was the first thing I said when I regained my voice. She gave back what you took from me."

I turn back to him, then cup the back of his neck and squeeze. But then my eyes catch on a blue photo album perched on his kitchen table. It looks out of place in the nearly empty room. My curiosity piqued, I abandon the pedophile and head for that album.

A gold trim lines the edges, but the front displays no label. I open it and flip through a few pages of old family photos. Maybe his parents and siblings? Scenery pictures slide by—some mountains, a little bird in a tree. But when I turn a few more pages, the images take a sudden turn.

My muscles tighten in waves beneath my skin, and goosebumps rise. From the very inside out I'm horrified by what I'm seeing.

Children.

So many children.

And worse, the little dinosaur backpack and matching lunchbox stares back at me from one of them. *My* little dinosaur backpack and matching lunchbox.

A fucking trophy.

I rip the photo from the album and stuff it into my pocket. As I keep flipping, I see more, and they only get worse. Some of them feature crying children. Some of them show him—

I rip a few from the pages and keep them in my hand as I return to the chair in the living room.

"You never stopped, did you? You never stopped

because *I* didn't stop you." The gravity of those words nearly sends me into insanity. My fear of speaking out against him let him go on to hurt all these other children.

Who knows how many voices he's stolen?

"Tell me their names," I snarl as I show him every fucking photo in my hand.

"Timothy," he says without looking up from the photo. I flip the picture. "David." I turn another. "Ryan."

I throw the rest around him, and they scatter on the floor. My vision closes around me until all I can see is the sick fucking man who ruined my life. I can't see Emmy anymore. I can't see her, but I can hear her crying. A kitchen knife slides toward me, and I realize Emmy is the one offering it to me.

"Be the monster you deserve to be," she says.

I look at the knife. I could. It would be so easy. But much like when we looked down at Jessie in that fire, something doesn't feel right about a quick death. It's too simple. Too easy. I have a better idea.

Instead of killing him, I toss him back on the ground and sit beside his head. He flails and screams as I put the tip of the knife against his forehead. I brand him with the letters that he deserves to carry forever. For eternity. Even in hell. Blood streams across his face as I finish the four letters that would indicate what this man did for the rest of the life he has left. I lay the pictures around him.

"Oh, that's gonna leave a scar," Emmy says through a sniffle. "I already know what you have planned next."

Her phone drops into my hand, saving me from having to search for mine, and I dial three numbers. When the operator answers, I give the address and the nature of this man's crimes, and then I hang up. They have all the evidence they need in that photo album, and when the other guys see that blazing all-caps brand on his forehead, they'll know exactly what he is.

PEDO

I grab Emmy and kiss her. "Let's go."

We wait at a bus stop a little way up the street. We can still see his house from here, and we get to enjoy every moment of his arrest. It's just a shame we won't get to see his eventual torture and death. I hope it's painful. As much as I wanted to see him die in front of me, he won't leave prison alive, and that feels more cathartic than killing him.

I pull Emmy into my chest, and I let myself cry hard for the first time in a long time. I take the photo of myself from my pocket—the only image I didn't leave behind. The ache in my gut intensifies at the very fact it exists. That he's kept it all these years.

I pull my brother's Zippo from my pocket, light a cigarette, and turn the flame to the photo before Emmy can see the true depravity of the image. It ignites, burning until I can no longer escape the heat. I let it fall to the sidewalk and turn to ash in front of us.

"Goodbye," I sign to that part of myself. The part of my life I so desperately wanted to leave behind. And then I kiss Emmy, my forever tomorrow. The part of my life that I never want to lose. Because I may have saved Jessie's girl, but she saved me too.

Thanks for reading! If you want to check out something a little less heavy, try the Slaycation series of dark rom-coms! Start with *Sinners Retreat*: Books2read.com/SinnersRetreat

If you want to take a darker roadtrip, check out all of my dark hitchhiker romance standalones in my Ride or Die series! These can be read in any order!

Hitched: Books2read.com/Hitched
Along for the Ride: Books2read.com/MFMHitchhiker
Driving my Obsession: Books2read.com/DrivingmyObsession
Across State Lines: Books2read.com/AcrossStateLines
Don't Stop: Books2read.com/Dont-Stop

Here are more dark-lite books you can check out!

Stranger Session: Books2read.com/StrangerSession
Her Fantasy: Books2read.com/HerFantasy
Last Mistake: Books2read.com/LastMistake
Protect Me: Books2read.com/ProtectMeNovella
Dark Decisions (Interactive):
Books2read.com/DarkDecisions
Morally Grey: Books2read.com/MorallyGrey
Edge of Sin: Books2read.com/EdgeofSin

Ready to go pitch-black?
Captured (banned as an ebook and audiobook):
Books2read.com/Capturedbook
Never Let Go: Books2read.com/NLG

CONNECT WITH LAUREN

Don't miss a thing from Lauren Biel! Check out all of her books, social media connections, and other important information at Campsite.bio/LaurenBielAuthor and Lauren Biel.com

ACKNOWLEDGMENTS

To my VIP gals (Jessie, Nikita, Lexi, Grace, and Kim), thank you for always being there for me.

Thank you to my husband, who is my own heart person. I would be nowhere without your support.

Whitney (Bayside Books) and Kelsey, forever "mayo" bonded best friends.

Brooke, my editor, you're more than just my best friend. You're my partner in crime. Thank you for always making my books the best they can be.

Hey, Mom! Here's another shoutout. Hi! ;)

I have to give a huge shoutout to Rick Springfield, who will likely never see this. Thanks for creating the backing track for the endless hours it took to write this book. I may or may not have had "Jessie's Girl" on repeat. Don't judge me. It's an excellent song.

Thank you to my valued Patrons. Your contribution helped make this book happen:

Stalker Chelle, Kari S, Scarlet, Kindra S, Jamie R, Destiny W, Cristen K, Dawn W, Misty, Kari L, Kelly S, Kim K,

Keasha M, Krysta, Stephanie C, Candice, Renee, Britt H, Elissa Z, Christina, Joanna H, Nicole K, Emma S, Megan P, Erin R, Stephanie F, Sabrina B, Melissa C, Melanie M, Stephanie M, Brandie H, Jennifer T, Brittany R, Jessica K, Renate E, Katie R, Rachel E, Brittany A, Laura, Laci B-P, Natalie V, Lisa R, Jessica P, Daphney G, Samantha H, Nalani P, Katina V, Deanna R, Liz M, Caitlin B, Kris, Kerry-Anne, Enchanted Owl, @ericanailstheplot, Megan P, Kassandra R, Lisapooh98, Jenna J, Ranae G, Veronica M, Alyssa S, Jessika W, Ashley S, Elvira, Amber C, Morgan C, Elle (Queen of Smut), AdorablyFeral_Reads, SamAndBig-DaddyD, Raquel O, SimplyDevine, Hollie C, Samantha F, Tanja, KitKatLaughAttack, Heather B, Laura F, Megan L, Leslie Mae, Ashley S, Kaat, Lauren.loves2read, Kimberly G, A.Reads, Danielle M, Danielle N, Sunshine_the_Bookie, Sara M, Harley B, Heather M, Bonnie F, Marguerite, Courtney R, Vikki S, Amanda T, Lisa W, Nicholetta88, Emily S, SerenaLorraine, Just Jen Here, Briyanna M, Gini R, Charmaine B, Michelle, Christy P, Callie K, Arnica S, Maxine T, Leslie W, Smitty, Brooke, Anna S, Shelby F, Tiannah J, Sharee S, Courtney P, Kristiana B, Vero A, Sara S, Samantha R, Jessica G, Kimberly S, Tabitha F, JesStenger, Nineette W, BoneDaddyAshe

ALSO BY LAUREN BIEL

To view Lauren Biel's complete list of books, visit: https://laurenbiel.com/laurenbielbooks/

ABOUT THE AUTHOR

Lauren Biel is the author of many dark romance books, with several more titles in the works. When she's not working, she's writing. When she's not writing, she's spending time with her husband, her friends, or her pets. You might also find her on a horseback trail ride or sitting beside a waterfall in Upstate New York. When reading her work, expect the unexpected. To be the first to know about her upcoming titles, please visit www.LaurenBiel.com.